The ROCK HOUND MYSTERY

The ROCK HOUND MYSTERY

MARY DUPLEX

Pacific Press Publishing Association
Boise, Idaho
Oshawa, Ontario, Canada

Edited by Jerry D. Thomas
Designed by Tim Larson
Cover and inside art by Georgina Larson
Typeset in 11/13 Century Schoolbook

Library of Congress Cataloging-in-Publication Data:
Duplex, Mary H.
   The rockhound mystery / Mary Duplex
       p.   cm.
   Summary: When the long-gone grandson of an elderly neigh-
bor returns, three young rockhounds become concerned about
mysterious and alarming things that begin to happen next door.
   ISBN 0-8163-1130-7
   [1. Mystery and detective stories. 2. Old age—Fiction. 3.
Oregon—Fiction. 4. Afro-Americans—Fiction. 5. Rocks—Collec-
tors and collecting—Fiction.] I. Title.
PZ7.D9262R0   1993
[Fic]—dc20   92-32971
                                                      CIP
                                                       AC

93 94 95 96 97 ● 5 4 3 2 1

Contents

Dedication

This one is for all of our budding rockhounds.

Chapter One

The Rockhounds

Casey Hilliard crouched behind the thick shrub near the porch steps and peeked out. So far, so good. His cousin Josie was nowhere in sight. Casey stayed hidden for another minute. You could never tell about Josie. Just because she was eleven too, and he was the only cousin her age, she stuck to him like a burr. What a pain! To make matters worse, she was spending the whole summer with them.

His mother, his older sister, Sharon, and his little brother, Toby, were down at the lake, swimming and playing on the beach. Josie had been out on the float when he slipped away. He couldn't see her now, but on such a hot day, Josie was probably more interested in keeping cool than tagging around after him.

The coast was still clear. Casey sprinted for the back steps and tiptoed across the screened-in back porch. He peered into the hall. Nobody was there. He dashed into the kitchen, snatched the phone off the wall, and dialed the number of his best friend, Myca Jordan.

Myca lived next door, but Casey wasn't taking any chances on being seen crossing the yard. "Mom says I can go. Come right away," he said in a low voice when Myca answered the phone.

"I'll meet you out front in two minutes," Myca said, and hung up.

Casey grabbed his rock bag from the cupboard on the porch. He made it as far as the corner of the house before Josie caught up with him.

"Where are you going?" Josie demanded.

"None of your business," Casey answered, wondering how she got dressed so fast. "Why don't you go for a swim with Sharon?"

"I already did. Now I want to go with you."

Sometimes, Casey wished they'd never moved here to the lake. He folded his arms across his chest and glared at her. "Well, you can't. Myca and I are going rockhounding with Mr. Beckerman. So get lost."

Josie put her hands on her hips and glared back at him. "I will not. And you can't make me. If you don't let me come, I'll follow you anyway," she threatened. "I know Mr. B. lives right over there on the other side of the hedge. I talked to him a lot of times last year by the beach, and he's nice. He won't mind if I come along."

Casey pressed his lips tight together and scowled his fiercest scowl. He knew it wasn't going to do any good to argue with her. Josie's hair was as red as his, and she was just as stubborn. But he wasn't going to tell her she could come with him and Myca.

"Beat it!" Casey snarled. He turned on his heel and stalked off, hoping she'd go away. No such luck. Josie was right behind him.

Myca, tall and thin, with skin the color of rich milk chocolate, was waiting at the edge of the driveway. "How come she's here?" he asked, motioning to Josie.

"She thinks she's my shadow." Casey slid a dark look at Josie and turned his back on her. "If we ignore her, maybe she'll go away."

"I will not! I'm coming too."

"You and Mr. Beckerman are the lucky ones," Casey muttered, hoping Josie would get tired and leave. "The only relative Mr. B. has is a grandson he hasn't seen for about twelve years. And you don't have any relatives at all. But me"—Casey clamped a hand to his bony chest—"I have relatives by the dozen. The lake and the Hotel Hilliard," he flung his other hand toward the house, "attract them like bare arms attract mosquitoes."

"Now hold on there, I never said I didn't have any kinfolk," Myca told him. "Most of them live down in New Orleans. But one of these days somebody will come for a visit and find out what a great place Oregon is. Then, look out!" Myca threw his arms up and jumped back in mock surprise. "There's gonna be Jordans all over the place."

Josie laughed. "See, not everybody is as mean as you, Casey."

Casey ignored her and turned to Myca. "Let me see the new rock you found. What is it?"

"I'm hoping it's a geode, but it could be a thunderegg." Myca held out a lumpy round rock about the size of a tennis ball.

"Could be either one." Casey took the rock and turned it over in his hands. "But I think it's a thunderegg."

"Geodes? Thundereggs? Let me see." Josie snatched the rock out of Casey's hand. "Looks like a plain old rock to me."

"Well, it's not." Casey grabbed it back.

"A geode is hollow in the center, and it's lined with crystals. Some of the crystals are amethyst and some are smoky quartz. But a thunderegg is solid agate inside. There are all kinds of colors and patterns," Myca explained.

Josie looked at the rock with new interest. "How can you tell?"

"You have to test 'em," said Myca.

"Show me what it looks like inside," said Josie.

Myca gave her a sheepish grin. "I'm afraid I'll break it. Geodes have a thin shell on the outside, and if you hit 'em too hard they break into a hundred pieces."

"That's why Myca is waiting until we get over to Mr. Beckerman's," said Casey. "He knows all about rocks."

"He surely does," Myca agreed. "Mr. B. is the best rockhound around here. He's been teaching us all about rocks. Let's get on over there; I'm itching to see the inside of this rock myself." Myca turned and started down the driveway.

"Mr. B. has the best collection of thundereggs in the whole state. They are the official rock of Oregon," Casey added.

"That's a dumb name for a rock," said Josie. "Why do you call it a thunderegg?"

Casey heaved a big sigh. "We didn't name it that. The Indians did a long time ago. It's Indian folklore. Mr. B. told us about it. He said in ancient times the Indians believed that when the thunder spirits of Mount Jefferson and Mount Hood got mad at each other they would grab the eggs from the thunderbird's nest and throw them at each other. The Indians found these rocks all over the place, so they called them thundereggs."

"That's interesting," said Josie. "But it's not really true."

"Of course not!" For a minute Casey had forgotten what a pain she could be. "The thundereggs were made when volcanoes erupted thousands of years ago."

They turned in by Mr. Beckerman's mailbox and made their way up his long, curving driveway. The big old Victorian house with its gables and tall chimneys, set back among the shrubs and trees, seemed to doze in the hot morning sun.

Josie stopped to stare. "Boy, this house is really old."

"It's the oldest house on the lake," said Casey. "Mr. B.'s family built it, before he was born, as a summer home. But he's lived in it year-round for a long, long time."

The house didn't look the least bit rundown or spooky. Mr. B. had given it a fresh coat of paint last spring. The bright sun glaring off the white walls made the wide porches look even deeper in shadows. They couldn't tell if Mr. B. was in his favorite chair, where he liked to look out over the lake, until they got closer. He wasn't.

Myca looked around. "I don't see him anywhere, do you? I surely do hope he hasn't forgotten about going rock-hounding with us."

Casey shook his head. "Mr. B. never forgets anything. Maybe he's out in his workshop."

"Rockhound. Sounds like some special breed of dog," said Josie, as they followed the white gravel path that curved around past tall shrubs and trees to the old carriage house.

"It's a name for folk who go looking for rocks," said Myca.

Mr. B. used half of the carriage house for a garage. The other half he had turned into a workshop for his rock collection and projects. He had rock-cutting machines and polishing machines. Even at this distance, they could hear the familiar clatter of rocks tumbling in the drum of the small electric rock polisher. Mr. B. kept it running most of the time, filled with pretty stones and pebbles Toby found and brought to Mr. B. to be polished.

"Hello, there," Mr. B. called. "Ready to go, are ya?"

At the sound of his voice, Casey looked up. Mr. B. was old, in his seventies, but Casey wasn't a bit surprised to see him up on the ridge of the steep roof. He stood there as straight and slim as a lodgepole pine, his white hair blowing in the breeze. He was wearing a pair of jeans, a blue work shirt with the cuffs turned back, and a pair of old red, high-topped tennis shoes.

"Hi, Mr. B.," Casey called back, squinting up at him.

"Hey, Mr. B.," Myca called too.

"What are you doing up there?" Josie shouted.

"Enjoying the view." Mr. B. shaded his eyes with one hand and peered off into the distance like an explorer scanning the horizon. "I can see clear across the lake from up here. Should have brought my binoculars. Then I could tell what the folk over at the picnic grounds are having for lunch."

"You coming down soon?" Myca asked, trying not to sound impatient.

Mr. B. chuckled. "Found something, did ya?" He held up a couple of new shingles and a hammer. "Got a little more repair work to do; then I'll be right down."

He walked along the ridge with his eyes on the roof as if he were looking for something. Then he took a few steps down the steep roof and braced himself with one foot. Tearing out an old shingle, he replaced it with a new one. He stood up and walked down the roof to the ladder as sure-footed as a mountain goat.

"Why are you repairing the roof now?" Josie asked.

"Best time to fix a leaky roof is when the sun is out," Mr. B. said when he came down. "Don't get wet that way." Josie giggled.

"Now let's see what you've got there," he said, turning to Myca.

"I hope it's a geode," said Myca, holding out the rock. "I found it over on Sawmill Creek Road where the road crew widened that curve."

Mr. B. nodded as he studied the rock. "New road cut is a likely place to do a little rockhounding. No telling what you're apt to turn up." His blue eyes twinkled as he said, "I suppose you're wanting to see what this thing looks like inside."

"Yes, sir, I surely would!" Myca was grinning and bouncing from one foot to the other.

"Well, now, let's see what kind of rockhound you're getting to be." Mr. B. opened the door of the workshop. "Come on in."

Chapter Two

Welcome Back

Mr. B. adjusted the rock-cutting machine and clamped Myca's rock into place. "It's going to take a while to make the cut," he said. "You can take a look around if you want. I'm going to crate up some of my craft projects. I have to deliver them to the gift shops at Lloyd Center in Portland tomorrow."

Myca didn't wait for a second invitation. He never missed a chance to have a look at Mr. B.'s geode collection. Josie, her eyes big and eager, moved slowly along the shelves that lined three walls. They were filled with specimens, each one carefully labeled with the name of the rock, the place it was found, and the date.

"I didn't know there were this many colors of quartz," Josie said, bending to look at each rock and read the labels.

Casey didn't have to read the labels. He knew them all by heart. "That's only the beginning," he said, and led her on to the next group. "Take a look at these."

There were jasper in rich shades of brown and petrified wood streaked with browns and blacks and tans. Light green olivine was sandwiched between layers of honeycombed brown. Next were pale opal and jade. Before they were halfway down the row, Josie squealed and dashed ahead of Casey.

17

"What are these?" Josie cried, leaning over another of Mr. B.'s collections. "I've never seen rocks as pretty as these before."

"They're thundereggs," Casey answered. "Mr. B. cut them all in half to show the patterns and colors of their solid agate centers." Some were streaked with yellow and orange, others with browns and creams. Still others had bars of reds and pinks and lavenders. Eye agates had rings of pale blue around circles of white that enclosed the dark centers. They reminded Casey of wide-open, frightened eyes.

Some of the bigger thundereggs looked like fantasy landscapes, dark silhouettes on creamy backgrounds. Others had faces and shapes of animals.

Casey never got tired of looking at all of them. But Josie was like a kid in a toy store. She rushed from one display to another. Finally, Josie spotted the collection Hal Beckerman, Mr. B.'s grandson, had left behind so long ago.

"Hey, Casey, come over here," she called. "What is that?" she asked, pointing to a bright blue translucent rock the size of a grapefruit that had been cut in two and polished.

"A blue thunderegg." Casey ran his fingers over the polished surface of the stone. "I keep looking, hoping I'll find one like it."

"And take a look at that dark purple geode," Myca pointed out. "Isn't that something?"

"It's beautiful," Josie agreed. "But what can you do with them? I mean, besides put them on a shelf and look at them?"

"Come on, and I'll show you," said Casey. He led her back across the room to the long wide bench where Mr. B. kept his finished work.

"This is what Mr. B. does with some of his rocks."

"Oh, wow!" Josie's eyes grew bigger and bigger as she circled the bench, looking at the clocks set in polished rock, the paperweights, and the matching pairs of bookends cut from the same thunderegg. One pair had a fantasy landscape outlined in the rock, dark colors against a background of marbled tan and cream. Another pair had the image of a cougar drinking from a pale blue translucent pool.

"They are all so beautiful! I can't believe they are rocks." Josie reached out and ran her fingers over the highly polished, glossy finishes. Each piece felt glassy smooth to the touch.

"Look at these blue sun catchers!" Casey picked up one and held it up to the sun streaming through the window. The curling white swirls in the bright blue looked like clouds in a summer sky. Mr. B. had cut the whole thunderegg in thin slices then drilled a small hole near the edges and attached wires to hang them up.

"Where did you find this one?" Casey asked, holding up a slice. "I want to find one like it. Will you take us there today?"

"That shade of blue is hard to come by around here," Mr. B. said, picking up an empty crate. "You'll have to talk your dad into taking you camping up in the Ochoco Mountains. Over Crook County way. That's where the best blue thundereggs come from. I've found some real beauties up there."

Casey shook his head. "Summertime is my dad's busiest season. He'll never have time to take us camping. Anyway, we have too much company to go anywhere in the summer."

"My dad can't take us either," said Myca. "Not now that the Real Cajun Cookin' Restaurant is starting to do a lot of business."

Mr. B. rubbed a hand over his clean-shaven chin and thought for a minute. "Well, now, come to think of it, I know a place not far from here. I've found some fair blue thundereggs there. The color isn't as bright, but they're worth bringing home. As soon as Myca's rock is finished, we'll get our little rockhounding expedition on the road."

Myca reached over and picked up a piece of geode. Glued to the sparkling amethyst crystals was a small pewter figure of an old prospector leading his mule. "Take a look at this, Josie."

"That's pretty, but I like this one better." She picked up a pewter bear standing tall on its hind legs and mounted on a piece of smoky quartz. Josie looked at it closely and said, "Mr. B., how do you polish all these little pieces of crystal and make them pointed?"

Casey hid his smile behind his hand, but Mr. B. looked at Josie over the crate between them with a straight face and said, "I don't. Nature makes them that way."

"Oh, I get it! You just crack them open, and they're ready to use." Josie sounded pleased with herself.

"Something like that," Mr. B. agreed. "The trick with a geode is to open it without smashing it to pieces. Come on over here, and I'll show you what I mean." The sound of the rock-cutting machine changed to a faster whine. Mr. B. reached over and turned it off as he went by. Josie followed along behind him, talking a mile a minute.

Casey glanced over at Myca and shook his head. "We could be on our way by now if she would stop asking questions."

Myca grinned. "You have to ask questions to get answers. We asked him a lot of questions too. Still do."

Mr. B. was showing Josie the huge half of an amethyst geode, big enough for her to sit in, when a car pulled up outside. He turned and glanced out the door. An old Toyota with a dented front fender stopped in front of the garage. Mr. B. moved to the doorway and waited as a young man wearing mirrored sunglasses and a short dark beard got out of the car. He had dark wavy hair and well-developed muscles under his black T-shirt. His jeans were ragged at the knees, and he had on a pair of dirty white sneakers. Casey had never seen him before. Maybe he was just a customer looking for something special, he thought.

When he was a few feet away, the man stopped. "Hello, Gramps," he said, a big smile spreading across his face.

Mr. B. sucked in a big breath and clutched at the hand railing by the step. He tipped his head a little to one side and said in a low voice, "Hal? Hal, is that you?"

"It's me, Gramps." Hal took off his sunglasses, and his smile widened into a grin. "Don't tell me I've changed that much." His eyes were brown like Mr. B.'s, and he was an inch or so taller.

"You've grown some since I saw you last." Mr. B. had a hard time getting the words out. "You were just a boy when you left here."

"I was eleven," said Hal. "And you were sixty-three."

Mr. B. took a few steps toward him, and Hal met him halfway. "You have changed," Mr. B. said, holding Hal at arm's length for a minute. "I might have walked right by you on the street without knowing you."

"Twelve years is a long time." Hal smiled and rubbed his fingers over the beard that covered the lower half of his face. "And I guess this makes a difference too. But you haven't changed, Gramps. You look just the same."

Suddenly, they were laughing and hugging and pounding each other on the back. Casey had seen his dad and uncles do that when they hadn't seen each other for a long time. Then, Mr. B. had to get out his bandanna and wipe his eyes. That's when he remembered Casey and Myca and Josie standing there.

Beaming with joy, Mr. B. put his arm around Hal's shoulders and said, "This is my grandson, Hal Beckerman. I've been telling you about him. Hal, this is Casey Hilliard, and Myca Jordan, my neighbors and a couple of budding rockhounds." Mr. B. reached over and patted Josie on the shoulder. "And this little lady is Josie McCawley, Casey's cousin. She's taking a mighty big interest in rocks too. Another rockhound, I suspect."

Josie grinned up at him. "I can't wait to find some rocks and start a collection of my own."

"Glad to meet all of you." Hal gave them a big, friendly smile and turned to Mr. B. "Gramps, have you still got my rock collection?"

Mr. B.'s eyes lighted up. "I sure do. It's still in the same place. Haven't moved a pebble of it since you've been gone." Mr. B. stepped back into the workshop and motioned for Hal to follow. "Go ahead and take a look at it. You know where it's at."

Hal stepped inside and stopped to look around, taking in the whole shop with quick, darting eyes. "This place sure brings back memories. I could spend hours in here. But if you don't mind, I think I'll look around later. It's been a long drive, and my throat is as dry as dust. We'll have plenty of time to catch up on the past while I'm here."

"How long are you going to stay?" Mr. B.'s back stiffened a little, as if he were bracing himself for bad news.

"A couple of weeks. Maybe a little longer, if you'll have me." That crooked grin spread across Hal's face again.

"Have you!" Mr. B. shouted. "Why, for years I've been praying you'd come back. I'd like nothing better than for you to stay here for good."

"Me too, Gramps. But I've got another year of college waiting for me when I get back. So we'll have to settle for a visit."

"While you're here, we're going to enjoy every minute." Mr. B. put a hand on Hal's shoulder. "Let's go over to the house, and I'll rustle up some lemonade."

"Sounds like old times. Your lemonade was always the best on a hot day." Hal moved toward the door.

"You kids must be thirsty too," Mr. B. said as he closed

the door to the workshop. "Come on, I'll fix enough for everybody."

It was easy to see Hal's surprise visit had driven all thought of the rockhounding trip out of Mr. B.'s mind. "Thanks, but we'd better be going," said Casey. When Myca and Josie just stood there, Casey nudged them with his elbows. "We have to go."

"Yeah, we have to go," said Josie.

"We'll see you later," said Myca.

Hal looked relieved. "Nice meeting you."

Mr. B. raised one hand in a wave. "Come back anytime." He turned and walked away with Hal.

"What did you tell him that for?" Josie grumbled in a low voice as they picked up their packs and started across the yard. "Mr. B. was going to take us rockhounding."

"No, he wasn't," Myca said. "He forgot about it when Hal came."

"They've got a lot of talking to do, and they don't want us hanging around listening to every word," said Casey. "Didn't you see the look on Hal's face when he thought we were coming along?"

"But Mr. B. said he'd show me a good place to hunt for geodes." Josie kicked a pine cone and sent it flying across the lawn. "He was going to show me where to find a blue thunderegg."

Casey looked back over his shoulder. Mr. B. and Hal were standing on the lawn. Mr. B. pointed out something down by the lake, then out on his dock. Hal nodded and laughed with him. Casey had never seen Mr. B. so happy. He'd been waiting for Hal to come back for a long time.

"Let's take the shortcut," said Myca. They crossed the lawn to the hole in the hedge that separated Mr. B.'s place from the Hilliards'. The hole was a lot bigger than it had been last spring. "I forgot about my rock!" Myca started to turn back.

"Wait until tomorrow," said Casey. Before Myca could object, Casey said, "It will give us an excuse to come back. Maybe, by then, Mr. B. will be ready to go rockhounding. Hal might want to come along too."

"I'd rather see what the rock looks like now." Myca gazed back at the workshop for a minute, then shrugged. "Guess I can wait." He shoved his pack through the hedge ahead of him and wiggled through after it. Casey and Josie wiggled through after him.

"Why do we have to wait for Mr. B. to take us rock-hounding?" asked Josie. "Why can't we go by ourselves?"

"We could go to that place where you found your rock, Myca. Mr. B. said that was a good place to hunt," said Casey.

"I don't feel like going clear out there to Sawmill Creek Road," said Myca. "It's hot, and we might not find anything."

"But what if we did?" Josie grabbed Myca's arm, determined not to miss her first chance to go rockhounding. "If we find a good geode or a thunderegg, we can take it over and show it to Mr. B. Let's do it!"

"There might be some more good rocks out there." Myca took two long strides across the Hilliards' front lawn and stopped. "How about taking a lunch along? It's a long ride out to that road cut. And I'm getting hungry already."

"Good idea," Casey agreed.

"Be back shortly." Myca trotted across the driveway and vaulted over the low fence.

Chapter Three

Orders Are Orders

"Nobody said anything about riding bikes," Josie fumed as she stomped up the back steps. "You know I don't have a bike. You and Myca just don't want me to come along. You want to keep all the good rocks for yourselves."

"We do not! You can ride Sharon's bike. She never uses it anymore. Not since she got her driver's license." Casey let the screen door slam behind him and followed Josie into the kitchen. His mother was there making out a shopping list.

"Hi, Aunt Rose," Josie said.

"Hi, Mom." Casey headed for the refrigerator.

Rose Hilliard turned from the open cupboard in surprise. "Back so soon? Did Mr. Beckerman change his mind about taking you boys out?"

"Mr. Beckerman has company," Josie volunteered.

"Must be very important company," Sharon said, coming out of the laundry room with a basket full of beach towels.

"It's Hal Beckerman, Mr. B.'s grandson from back East." Casey added a jar of jam and a block of cheese to what he already had in his arms. He bumped the door shut with his hip and made it to the table without dropping anything. "Mr. B. didn't know he was coming."

"What a wonderful surprise for Mr. Beckerman," Mom

said. "He's been hoping for a long time that Hal would come for a visit."

"They were really happy to see each other," said Josie, opening the bread drawer to get out the bread.

"Ma, will you hand me the peanut butter, please?" asked Casey.

Mom frowned. "Casey, what are you doing? It isn't lunchtime yet."

"We're not going to eat now. It's for later. Since we can't go rockhounding with Mr. B., we decided to go over to Sawmill Creek Road and look in that new road cut. Myca found a good rock there."

"You are supposed to ask permission first," his mother reminded him. She opened another cupboard and sorted through it. "That's odd," she said, looking puzzled. "I know I saw a big jar of peanut butter in here day before yesterday. What could have happened to it?"

"Aunt Hazel used the last of it to make sandwiches to take with them on the trip home yesterday," Sharon told her mother. "Aunt Hazel said it was too expensive to eat in restaurants with four kids."

Mom sighed and added peanut butter to her list. "Anything else?" she asked, looking up.

"Bread," said Josie.

"And cheese," said Casey, slicing the last of the block into lopsided chunks.

Josie sorted through the last of the apples in the fruit basket on the counter and picked out three to add to their lunch. "If I find a big geode or a good thunderegg, I'm going to ask Mr. B. to show me how to make something out of it," she said as they started for the door.

Mom, her shopping list in hand, followed them out to the screened-in porch. "I don't want you kids over there bothering Mr. Beckerman while his grandson is here."

"But, Ma," Casey objected, "We're . . ."

"You are to stay away from Mr. Beckerman's unless you are invited." She shook a finger under Casey's nose. "Is that clear? Mr. Beckerman and his grandson need a lot of time to themselves while Hal is here. I don't want you kids hanging around over there. And that's an order." When Mom got that no-nonsense look on her face, Casey knew she wasn't going to budge, no matter what he said.

"OK." Casey let out his breath in a loud sigh so she would know he wasn't happy about the agreement. But Mom didn't seem to notice. She turned and went back into the house.

"Now how are we going to remind Mr. B. about the rockhounding trip?" said Josie.

Casey spread his hands and lifted his shoulders in a helpless shrug. "Orders are orders," he said.

It was almost two weeks before they saw Mr. Beckerman again.

Chapter Four

Bending the Rules

Casey and Myca spent most of their time showing Josie how to become a rockhound. They had finished with the road cut days ago and gone in search of better places. They had been poking around in the rubble at the bottom of the steep bank for almost an hour when Casey spotted a round, lumpy rock. He reached for it at the same time Myca did. Their heads came together with a loud thump! Casey straightened up, holding one hand to the top of his head. Myca staggered backward, rubbing his forehead. Then before either one of them could yell, "I saw it first!" Josie reached down and picked up the rock.

"Hey, no fair!" Myca protested.

"It's mine!" Casey yelled. "You got the last one!"

"I didn't say I was going to keep it." Josie turned the rock over and looked at it from all angles. She had learned almost as much about rocks in the last two weeks as they had since last spring. Josie wet one finger and rubbed over a spot on the rock. "Give me your rock hammer, and I'll test it," she said, holding out her hand to Casey.

"No way." Casey shook his head. "You might ruin it."

"Then you test it." Josie held out the rock.

Casey looked it over, then held it up to his ear and shook it hard. "It doesn't rattle, so it must be a thunдеregg." He started to put it in his pack.

"I don't believe you guys!" Josie exploded. "That's the fifth rock like that we've found, and we don't know what any of them look like inside. Why don't you just chip a little piece off each one so we can see what's under the ugly part?"

"I forgot my goggles," said Myca. "Can't chip rocks without 'em. Mr. B. will cut them open for us," said Myca. "He won't mind doing it."

Josie blew a strand of red hair out of her eyes and stuck her hands on her hips. "Well, I want to see what's inside of them. Let's go show them to Mr. B."

"You know we can't," Casey reminded her. "Mom said we couldn't go over to Mr. B.'s while Hal was there unless we were invited."

"But we were invited," said Josie. "Remember? Mr. B. said to come back anytime. That's being invited, isn't it?"

"Mr. B. always says that," said Myca.

Casey thought for a minute. A slow smile spread across his face. "Mom told Josie and me we couldn't go over there without an invitation. But she didn't say anything about you. You want to bend the rules a little?"

Myca grinned. "Don't mind if I do. What are we waiting for?" They hopped on their bikes and started down the road.

"I heard something mighty strange in the restaurant yesterday," Myca told them as they rode along. "Two men were sitting in the back booth near where I was filling salt and pepper shakers for my mom. They were talking about a big old house full of antiques down by the lake. Ten rooms filled with the same furnishings it had when the house was built around the turn of the century. And they're fixing to buy up a lot of the furniture. You know about any houses like that?"

"It sounds like Mr. B.'s house," said Casey. "But it can't be. He'd never sell his furniture or anything else in the house."

When they reached Mr. Beckerman's driveway, Casey stopped and said, "Josie and I will wait here. You take the rocks and show them to Mr. B." Casey dug two rocks out of his rock bag and handed them to Myca.

"I'll be back directly." Myca stowed the rocks in his own bag and rode off down the tree-shaded drive.

Casey and Josie picked a spot in the shade and settled down to wait. But before they could get comfortable, Myca was back.

"Wasn't Mr. B. home?" Josie asked, getting to her feet.

"He's there." Myca had a strange look on his face. "There's something mighty funny going on. Come on, you have to see for yourselves. It's Mr. B. I think there's something wrong with him." Myca turned and pointed. "This way is fastest." Casey and Josie parked their bikes in the shade of a huge oak tree halfway down the drive and hurried after Myca on foot. He led them across the gardens to where they could see the back lawn from behind a clump of bushes.

"There he is," Myca whispered.

Casey separated the branches and looked out. "I've never seen Mr. B. act like that before. What's wrong with him?"

"I saw a man act like that in the city park once," said Josie, peering out on the other side of Casey. "He was staggering around, muttering to himself like that. Only he was clutching a bottle in his arms, not a picture frame. My dad said he was drunk."

"Mr. B. isn't drunk," said Casey. "He never drinks. There's something wrong with him. Come on, we better go help him before he hurts himself."

"I wonder what happened to Hal?" said Myca as they pushed past the bushes. "Do you suppose he left for home already?"

"If he were still around, he'd be out here helping Mr. B.,"

said Casey. He reached the old man in time to keep him from falling. "Mr. B., are you all right?" Casey took his arm, and Myca grabbed the other.

At the sound of Casey's voice, Mr. B. turned his head and tried to focus his bleary eyes on Casey. He was all excited and kept muttering the same thing over and over. "What's he saying?" asked Josie.

"I don't know, but we'd better get him in the house and call 911," said Casey. They turned him around and started for the house.

"Are you on some kind of medication?" Josie asked, walking backward in front of him. "Did you eat something that didn't agree with you?" The picture slipped from his trembling grasp as he tried to shove it at her. Josie caught it and gave it back to him.

Suddenly the door flew open, and Hal rushed out. "Here, I'll take care of him." Hal brushed Casey and Myca aside and put a strong arm around Mr. Beckerman's waist. Mr. B. struggled and fought, muttering the same words over and over again. But he was no match for Hal.

"What's wrong with him?" Josie asked.

Hal gave them a big smile. "I'm afraid he's had a drop too much to drink. He's been doing a little celebrating. Gramps will be fine after he's had a little nap." Hal hustled Mr. B. inside and closed the door firmly behind them.

They were too surprised to say anything. They stood there staring at the closed door for a minute, then turned away. Nobody said anything until they reached their bikes.

Casey looked back. "Can you believe that Hal, trying to make us believe Mr. B. had too much to drink?"

"I was right in front of him, and he didn't smell awful like that man in the park did," said Josie.

"Did you see the way Mr. B. looked?" said Myca. "I've never seen him look so bad. His hair all snarly and whiskers on his chin. Something isn't right."

"What should we do?" asked Josie, turning to look back too.

"Let's tell my mom," said Casey. "She'll know what to do."

"You might get into trouble for being over here," said Myca.

"I'd rather get into trouble with Mom than have something happen to Mr. B.," said Casey.

They turned their bikes around and headed for home.

Chapter Five

Bird's Eye View

They dropped their bikes and rushed up the back steps. Casey yanked the screen door open. Josie and Myca were right behind him when he burst into the kitchen. It was empty.

"Mom!" Casey yelled. "Where are you?"

"In here," his mother answered from the living room. "Now that my cousin Ed and his family are gone, I'm enjoying a few minutes of peace and quiet. You look upset," she said as they rushed into the room. "Is something wrong?"

"It's Mr. B." Suddenly they were all talking at once.

"Stop!" Mom put her hands up over her ears. "One at a time," she shouted. "I can't understand a word you're saying."

Josie was trying to explain what had happened, when a horn tooted in the driveway.

"Now, who can that be?" Mom glanced toward the window with a look of annoyance on her face.

Casey moved the curtain aside and looked out. "It's Uncle Wes and Aunt Dee and all their kids. It looks like they're planning to stay, Mom. Their station wagon is full of luggage. And there's another car right behind them."

"There must be some mistake!" Mom rushed to the

window and peered over Casey's shoulder. "Dee wrote and said they were taking the kids to Disneyland this year. Maybe they just stopped by to say Hello."

The doorbell rang. Before anyone could move, Uncle Wes's voice boomed through the front hall. "Anybody home?"

Mom crossed the room and paused to pat her hair into place.

"What about Mr. B.?" Casey called after her. "We haven't told you everything yet."

"You'll have to tell me later." Mom took a deep breath, forced a smile to her lips, and went to greet their guests. Casey and Josie and Myca followed her out into the hall.

"Wes! What a surprise. Dee wrote that you were off to Disneyland this year," Mom said.

"That is the plan," Wes Hilliard admitted. "But we're going to postpone the trip for a few days. Chet stopped by yesterday to talk about having a family reunion. It's been a long time since the whole Hilliard family has been together. And Tom is always the one who is too busy in the summer to get away. So this year we decided to bring the reunion to him."

"What . . . what about the rest of the families?" Mom had a sick-looking smile on her face.

Uncle Wes grinned. "Now don't you worry about a thing, Rose. Chet and Estelle and their kids came along with us. And I called Mom and Dad from my place. They'll be here in a little while. Libby is home from college, and she's coming with them." Uncle Wes moved toward the front door. "I'll start bringing in the luggage. You want us in the same rooms as last year?"

A couple of minutes later, the whole house was alive with people—kid-cousins running up and down the stairs yelling about who got to sleep where, adults milling around, all talking at once.

"Let's get out of here before we get trampled," Casey said

to Josie and Myca. They worked their way down the hall to the back porch and made their escape.

"What are we going to do about Mr. B.?" asked Myca when they found a corner of the yard all to themselves.

"We can't just leave him over there with that awful Hal," said Josie. "There's no telling what will happen to him if we do."

"We'll talk to Mom again when there aren't so many people around," said Casey. "She didn't understand what we were telling her before."

"With all these people, it's apt to be a mighty long time before you get your mother alone," said Myca. "Why don't we ride into town and tell my mom. She'll know what to do."

Suddenly the screen door banged open. Toby and the twins, Butch and Buddy, and the other cousins, all in bathing suits, came swarming down the steps. They were followed a minute later by Aunt Dee and Aunt Estelle.

"Casey," Mom called from the back steps. "Will you and Josie come here for a minute?"

"Now is our chance to talk to her alone," Casey said. They hurried across the patio.

"Casey, I hate to ask you to give up your room again," Mom said. "I can't imagine where your uncles thought we would put everyone."

"That's OK, Mom," Casey said. "I don't mind sleeping on the porch. Mom, about Mr. B. We think there is something wrong with him." They took turns explaining what had happened at Mr. Beckerman's earlier.

Mom listened carefully to each one in turn. When they were finished, she smiled. "I don't think Hal is trying to harm Mr. Beckerman. You kids mustn't jump to conclusions. From what you've told me, it does sound like Mr. Beckerman had too much to drink."

"Mom, Mr. B. has gone to our church every week since

we met him. You know he doesn't drink. Not ever," Casey insisted.

"Casey, nobody is perfect. Not even Mr. B. Now I'm sure there's nothing to be concerned about. I met Hal at the bank, and he seems very nice. He'll take good care of his grandfather." Mom turned to go back into the house. "Oh, one more thing," she said, turning to Josie. "Would you mind moving your things out of Sharon's room so I can put Libby in there? It will only be for a few days, I promise."

"I don't mind," Josie answered.

Mom smiled. "Thanks. That solves the problem of the adults. Now for the kids. Casey, will you get the tent out of the garage and set it up for me?"

"Sure. Just tell me where you want it," said Casey.

With one hand on her hip, Mom studied the back lawn carefully. She pointed to a grassy level place not far from the back steps. "Put the tent there. It will be out of the way and close enough to the house for anyone who needs to come in during the night." The phone began to ring, and Mom rushed to answer it.

"You want me to help you with the tent?" Myca asked.

Casey shook his head. "No. You go tell your mom about Mr. B. Maybe she'll believe us. My mom sure didn't."

"I'll be back directly and tell you what she said." Myca swung a long leg over his bike and headed for town.

"Do you think there's a chance Aunt Rose could be right about Mr. B.?" Josie asked as they walked toward the garage.

"No way," said Casey. "I hope he'll be all right tomorrow."

"Me too."

Casey opened the side door of the garage. "Now if I can remember where Dad put the tent."

They spent the next half hour looking through the dusty storage section of the garage before Casey remembered where the tent was stored. He had to move several boxes and a couple of plastic garbage bags of old clothing to get to the tent.

"How long has it been since you used that thing?" Josie asked as clouds of dust billowed up from the corner.

"Too long." Casey shoved another box out of the way and reached for the tent. "We haven't gone camping since we moved here." He found the bag of tent poles and handed them to Josie. "Here, you carry this; it's not heavy." Casey hoisted the tent to his shoulder and snagged a hammer off the wall on his way out of the garage.

"Is this where you want the poles?" Without waiting for an answer, Josie dumped the bag on the grass and dusted off her hands.

"That's close enough." Casey dropped the tent beside it. He knelt down and unfolded the tent until he found the plastic ground cover. He shook it out and handed one corner to Josie. "Here, help me lay this out." They spread the big sheet of plastic out on the spot his mother had picked. Then Casey put the tent in the middle of it. "We used to use this tent a lot before Dad was transferred and we bought this house," said Casey. "Sometimes we'd go on hiking trips up in the mountains. Or we'd travel along the coast highway and stop at some really great beaches. Now, we never get to do that stuff anymore."

"Casey Hilliard, you are such a complainer!" Josie gave him a punch on the shoulder. "Uncle Tom and Aunt Rose bought this place so you and Sharon and Toby could do all the fun things around here, and all you do is gripe." She threw one arm wide, taking in the lake and the surrounding woods and hills. "I wish my family lived here."

"You wouldn't think it's so great if you always had to do what somebody else wanted to do first," he said.

"Or had somebody else tagging along all the time?" Josie asked with a silly, lopsided grin.

Casey lifted one shoulder in a shrug. "Aw, you're not so

bad for a girl. At least you like to do the same things I do. And you don't complain about getting dusty and dirty."

Josie crawled across the flattened tent to smooth out a bunched-up fold. "Straighten your corner over there." She watched to make sure he did it right.

"Here, put these by the loops on your side." Casey handed her half of the tent pegs. "I'll start pounding these in the corner loops over here."

They took turns driving in the pegs. While Josie finished the last two, Casey laid out the metal poles.

"This tent is a lot easier to put up than ours," said Josie. They set the corner poles in place and slipped the ends into the top framework, then extended the corner poles until the tent was stretched taut. After they had unzipped the window flaps to let the breeze blow through, they both stepped back and looked the tent over.

"It looks straight to me," said Casey.

"It looks straight from this side too." Josie lifted the hair off her neck. "Putting up tents is hot work. After we tell Aunt Rose the tent is set up, let's put on our suits and go for a swim."

"I'll race you out to the float," said Casey.

"And I'll beat you." Josie grinned as they ambled across the porch and down the hall.

Casey and Josie found his mother upstairs putting fresh sheets on the other twin bed in Sharon's room.

"Finished already?" Mom brushed a strand of dark hair out of her eyes as she straightened up. "You've been so much help I really hate to ask, but would you mind getting the sleeping bags and pillows down from the attic for me? They're in the storage closet."

"Do you want all of them?" Casey asked.

"Yes, even the old ones. And hurry, Aunt Libby called a little while ago to say they are on their way."

Casey and Josie climbed the attic stairs. "It sure is hot up here," said Casey, fanning his face with his hand.

"Too hot to breathe. I'll open the window," said Josie.

"I'll have to help you. That window always sticks." Casey tapped the top of the lower window frame. "Grab it right here, and when I say go, push up hard."

The window held for a second, then suddenly slid open. Casey and Josie leaned out, breathing in the cool air.

"Hey, look! We've got a bird's eye view of Mr. B.'s backyard from up here," said Josie.

"Well, this bird is ready for a swim. Let's get . . ." The words died on Casey's lips when he saw Hal.

Chapter Six

Who Gets the Tent?

"Who is Hal talking to?" Josie leaned farther out the window.

"It's Mr. Sidel. He's been coming around Mr. B.'s every couple of months for over a year trying to get Mr. B. to sell his property. Mr. B. keeps telling Sidel that he isn't interested. But Sidel keeps giving Mr. B. his card and saying he'll be back in case Mr. B. changes his mind." Casey turned from the window. "Let's get the sleeping bags."

Josie watched the two men with interest, then said, "You know what it looks like? It looks like Mr. Sidel is pointing out all the best parts of Mr. B.'s property. But I don't think he likes the house."

"Who cares what he likes?" Casey dropped the sleeping bag he was holding and pulled another one from the shelf.

"Now they're shaking hands," Josie reported. "You don't think Mr. B. changed his mind, do you?"

Casey shook his head. "Not a chance."

"Hal acts like he's doing business with Mr. Sidel. He's signing some papers. I think they just made a deal," Josie reported.

"That's impossible!" Casey threw down the pillows and rushed to the window, craning his neck to see. "Hal can't sell Mr. B.'s house. It doesn't belong to him!"

"So what are you getting so upset about?" Josie gave Casey a poke in the ribs with her elbow. "Come on, it's too hot to stand around up here spying on the neighbors. Let's get those sleeping bags taken care of and go get wet."

There were too many sleeping bags and pillows to carry all at once. It was going to take forever to get them all downstairs.

"I have an idea," said Josie. "Let's pile the pillows and sleeping bags over there at the top of the steps. Then you go down to the bottom of the steps, and I'll toss them down to you. We'll do the same thing to get them downstairs."

"Good thinking!" Casey grabbed up a load of sleeping bags. It didn't take long to get them out of the attic.

Casey clattered downstairs to the bottom floor. "Toss them down," he called. By the time they had all of the sleeping bags downstairs, Mom had finished cleaning and preparing the bedrooms.

"Don't just leave those bags in the hall," she called down over the banister. "Take them out to the tent and lay them out in some kind of order." She looked as hot and damp as Casey felt.

Josie put her hands on her hips and blew a strand of damp hair off her forehead as she eyed the jumbled heap. "One more time," she said as she tucked a sleeping bag under each arm and grabbed one more by the cord that held it together.

"Yeah, once more." Casey picked up three more bags. They were on their way across the yard to the tent when Myca came back.

"What took you so long?" Casey asked.

"I haven't been gone that long." Myca held the tent flap back so they could carry the sleeping bags inside.

It was hot inside the tent. The smell of the warm canvas reminded Casey of the camping trips his family had taken. He breathed in the good smell as he dropped the bags and started to untie the cords.

"What did your mother say about Mr. B.?" Josie asked, unrolling one of the sleeping bags and spreading it out next to the far wall.

"I had to wait a while before I got a chance to talk to her," said Myca, helping Josie spread out the second bag next to the first. "The restaurant was crowded, and she was real busy. So I followed her out to the kitchen. Mama usually listens to me. But Mr. B. took Hal into all of the stores and shops and introduced him to everybody he knows, including my folks. After I told her about Mr. B., she said he was a fine, Christian man. But like the pastor says, the road to heaven is a rocky one. And even the best of folk dash their foot against the stones of temptation now and again. And she said that Hal was a nice young man. And for me to get along home and not go pestering Hal and Mr. B."

"I knew it," Josie fumed. "Grown-ups never listen to kids."

"Hal sure knows how to make friends with adults," Casey grumbled.

"That's not the only weird thing that happened today," said Myca. "You'll never guess who I passed coming out of Mr. B.'s driveway a little bit ago."

"Mr. Sidel—that guy who's been trying to buy Mr. B.'s property," said Casey.

Myca's mouth fell open. "How did you know that? Did you go over there without me?"

Casey shook his head. "We saw him and Hal out in the backyard from the attic window a little while ago."

"I thought Hal and Mr. Sidel were making a deal," said Josie. "But Casey says Mr. B. will never sell him the property. So Mr. Sidel was just wasting his time again. Casey, toss me that other pillow."

"Well, something good must have happened," said Myca. "Mr. Sidel had a big grin on his face when he drove away. Like somebody had just handed him a million dollars."

They heard a car door slam and voices calling from the driveway.

Casey glanced out the side window of the tent. "It's Gran and Grandpa and Aunt Libby," he said.

"Tom! Rose! We're here," Gran called. A minute later, Casey saw his mother in the driveway to greet them. "We would have been here earlier, but Libby had to make a last-minute change in plans." Aunt Libby was Dad's youngest sister. She was young and pretty, and Casey suspected the change in plans had something to do with a boyfriend.

"Sounds like more guests for the Hotel Hilliard," said Myca, grinning at Casey.

"A family reunion," said Casey. "It was my uncles' idea. "Mom's going crazy trying to figure out where to put everybody."

"Well, this tent will take care of six of them," said Josie. "Now that we've got it all ready, let's get out of here and go for that swim. I'm melting." As they stepped outside, the cousins came running up from the beach wrapped in soggy, sandy beach towels.

Megan was the first one to reach the tent. She poked her head inside to look around. "Hey, this is neat! Who gets to sleep here?"

Casey shrugged. "I don't know. Nobody said yet."

Cindy pushed the tent screen aside and barged in. "There are more girls than boys, so the girls get to have the tent. I get that sleeping bag over there by the window." She left a trail of sand and water across the canvas floor and sleeping bags.

Butch and Buddy and two of the boy-cousins pushed their way in. "Who gets to sleep in here?" Butch demanded.

"Yeah, who gets to?" his twin brother Buddy echoed.

"We do!" Cindy folded her arms across her chest and glared at him. "There are more girls than boys."

"There are not!" Butch yelled. "There are just as many guys as there are girls."

"Yeah, there are just as many guys," Buddy repeated.

"You can't count Stevie. He's too little," Cindy insisted.

The tent was suddenly filled with kids, shouting, arguing, pushing, and tracking sand and water everywhere.

"All of you get out of here!" Casey yelled above the commotion. They all ignored him. Somebody started a pillow fight. "Hey, cut it out!" Casey shouted, trying to break it up.

"Forget it," Josie yelled. "If they want to sleep in wet, sandy sleeping bags, that's their problem." Casey and Myca managed to work their way out the door without getting hit.

"I'm ready for a swim," Casey told Myca when they were far enough away from the tent to talk without shouting. "Want to come along?"

Myca grinned. "Best idea I've heard all day. I'll meet you down at the lake as soon as I get changed."

By the time Casey and Josie came out of the house and headed for the beach, someone had stopped the free-for-all in the tent.

"I wonder who won, the boys or the girls?" said Josie.

"Who cares?" said Casey. "I wonder if Mr. B. is really thinking about selling his house."

"You said Mr. B. loves that old house and he's lived there all his life. Why would he sell it?" asked Josie.

"I sure wish we could talk to him and get the answers to these questions," said Casey.

He ran across the hot sand and splashed ankle deep in the water. He moved along the shore until he was almost on Mr. B.'s side of the beach. From there, he could see past the end of the hedge and into Mr. Beckerman's yard. There was no sign of the struggle that had taken place earlier. The yard looked the same as ever. Maybe they had been imagining things. Hal was Mr. B.'s grandson. Why would he want to do anything to harm him?

"Go for it!" Myca yelled, sprinting across the beach.

"Race you to the float!" Josie splashed past, close on Myca's heels.

"Hey, wait for me!" Casey hit the water at a full run. The cold shock took his breath away as he went under. He sputtered to the surface, feeling cool and refreshed as he swam after Josie and Myca.

Casey forgot about Mr. B. while they practiced dives and cannonballs off the diving board. It wasn't until they swam back to shore and he saw Hal waiting for them on the beach that it all came flooding back again.

Chapter Seven

Something Funny Going On

"It looked like you were having fun out there. How's the water?" Hal said with a big, friendly smile as they waded out of the lake.

"The water is great," said Josie, picking up her towel and wrapping it around her shoulders. "Are you going for a swim?"

Hal shook his head. "No, I'm not much of a swimmer. I came over to thank you for helping me with Gramps today. I didn't mean to be rude to you earlier. I was so worried about Gramps, I forgot my manners."

"Is Mr. B. all right now?" asked Myca, shaking the sand off his towel and wiping the water from his face.

"I shouldn't tell you this. I know you're friends of his," said Hal, "but I think it's best to warn you. Gramps has been on a real drinking spree for the last few days. And he gets very violent at times." Hal took off his sunglasses and showed them his black eye. "Gramps packs a pretty mean wallop, so you kids better stay away until he's himself again."

Casey draped his towel around his neck. "How long is that going to be?" He had a funny feeling Hal wasn't telling them the truth.

"It might be a week, ten days." Hal spread his hands and

lifted his shoulders in a shrug. "I really don't know how long Gramps's drinking bouts last." He flashed his big smile again. "But I do know Gramps wouldn't want you to see him at his worst."

"When can we see him?" asked Myca.

"As soon as Gramps is back to normal, I'll let you know. Now, I'd better get back and see how he's doing. Thanks again for your help." Hal turned and hurried back up across Mr. Beckerman's yard.

They stood there silently and watched until he disappeared from view behind a clump of bushes. "Do you think maybe Mr. B. really does have a drinking problem?" Josie asked. "Hal's black eye was no fake."

"His black eye was real," Casey agreed. "But Hal is lying about how he got it. He wants us to stay away from Mr. B for some reason."

"How come you think that?" said Myca. "We all saw Mr. B., and he for sure wasn't himself. Something was mighty wrong with him."

"I know," said Casey. "It's the only explanation that makes any sense. That's what bothers me. We all know Mr. B. doesn't drink or do drugs. And he's never been angry or violent once since we've known him. But what else could it be?"

"Then you do think he was drinking?" asked Josie.

"That's what Hal wants us to think. Something funny is going on at Mr. B.'s that he doesn't want us to know about," Casey answered.

"Casey! Josie! Time for dinner," Aunt Libby called.

"Coming!" Casey yelled. They started up the lawn to the patio.

"Funny like what?" Josie asked.

"Like Mr. B. was fine until Hal showed up. We don't see Mr. B. for a couple of weeks and when we do, he's staggering around mumbling and clutching that picture."

"It was a picture of Hal in a cap and gown without a beard." Josie rubbed her towel over her wet hair.

"How do you know all that?" said Myca.

"I saw the picture when Mr. B. almost dropped it."

"Why would Mr. B. be packing Hal's picture around?" said Myca.

"If we could talk to Mr. B., he'd be able to tell us," said Casey.

"I suspect you're right about Hal not wanting us to talk to him," Myca said. "But what if Mr. B. is likely to do us some harm if we get close to him? From the look of Hal's eye, it's mighty chancy."

"I know we'd be taking a chance," said Casey. "But there are too many weird things going on."

"What can we do about it?" Josie asked. "Nobody paid any attention to us when we tried to tell them about Mr. B."

"That's because they all think Hal is such a great guy," said Casey. "We need to find out what he's up to."

"How are we going to do that?" said Myca.

"There are ways," said Casey. "I just haven't thought of any yet. First thing tomorrow, we're going to start getting some answers. But don't say anything until we know for sure what's going on."

"I'd better go home," said Myca.

The mixed aromas made Casey's mouth water. "No, stay and have dinner with us," he said. "We need time to figure out a plan."

"Are you sure your mother won't mind me staying for dinner?" asked Myca, when he saw all the people in the patio.

"With this crowd, Aunt Rose won't even notice you're here," said Josie. "Come on, let's get something to eat. I'm starved."

They joined the crowd near the serving table. Everyone bowed their heads while Dad asked the blessing. Casey added a silent prayer of his own, asking God to be with Mr. B.

"It all looks so good, I don't know what to try first," said Myca.

"Try a little bit of everything," said Josie, helping herself.

Casey found room on his heaping plate for a serving of baked beans, then looked around for a place to sit. The picnic table was filled with cousins. And the adults had taken over the lawn chairs. "Over here," Josie called from the back-porch steps.

"I forgot to call my mom to tell her where I am," said Myca, setting his plate down between Josie and Casey. "Watch my food so it doesn't get stepped on." He hurried into the kitchen.

After they had gone back for seconds and helped themselves to dessert, Josie asked, "Have you thought of a plan yet?"

"We need an excuse to go back over to Mr. B.'s without making Hal suspicious," said Casey.

They sat there on the steps for a long time, thinking. Suddenly Casey grinned. "I've got it! First thing in the morning, this is what we'll do."

Chapter Eight

Keeping the Peace

It was almost eight o'clock when the sun, shining through the tent window, woke Casey up. He stepped over the twins, Butch and Buddy, and his little brother, Toby, without waking them up. Then shuffling between Greg and Stevie, he crawled out of the tent. He hadn't figured on getting stuck sleeping out there with the boys. But he didn't have much choice when his mother decided the girls, including Josie, should sleep on the screened-in porch.

The way Cindy and Megan kept giggling half the night, it was a wonder anybody got any sleep. They might never have gone to sleep if Josie hadn't threatened to smother them both with pillows. Casey knew she wouldn't, and so did Cindy and Megan, but they finally quieted down.

The delicious aroma of pancakes met Casey as he climbed the back steps. He rushed upstairs to the bathroom to wash and get dressed. He had to wait his turn, and by the time he came back downstairs, the cousins were up, waiting to be fed.

"Did you sleep well?" his mother asked, cooking six pancakes on the electric griddle.

"I guess so," Casey said. "Can I have something to eat now?"

"Do you mind waiting for the next batch?" Mom asked with a smile. "These have all been spoken for." She lifted the pancakes and stacked them onto a platter. "Here," she said, handing it to him. "Take these out to Aunt Estelle so she can help the little ones fill their plates."

It was half an hour before Casey and Josie got to sit down at the picnic table and eat. By then, Myca was there waiting for them. They were just finishing up when Butch and Buddy raced around the corner of the house with Cindy right behind them.

"If you get to climb Goat Mountain, so do we, Butch Hilliard!" Cindy announced hotly.

Butch swung around and gave her a disdainful look. "Girls can't climb up there. It's too steep. Besides, there are rattlesnakes up there this long." He stretched his arms out as far as they would go. "You'd scream your head off if you saw even a baby one."

"Yeah, you'd scream your head off," his twin brother, Buddy, echoed.

"We would not! Girls aren't afraid of any old snakes. Are we, Megan?" Cindy asked. Megan shook her head, but she didn't look like she meant it.

"See, I told you." Cindy put her hands on her hips and stuck her face up close to Butch's. "We can climb better than you, and we'll get to the top before you do."

Butch leered at her. "No, you can't! You wouldn't get halfway up before you'd be begging to come back."

"Yeah, you wouldn't get halfway," Buddy agreed. By now all the cousins were watching with interest.

"We will too!" Cindy's face was turning red. "We'll climb clear to the top. Just wait and see."

"Well, you can't go with us!" Butch yelled, breathing hard.

Casey was beginning to wonder if he should break it up before it turned into a real fight. He was getting up from the table, when his father heard the argument and came to the rescue.

"Here, what's all the ruckus about?" Tom Hilliard was a big man. He put his hands on his knees and bent down. "Sounds pretty serious." Cindy and Butch both started talking at once, each one trying to outshout the other.

"Whooo! Enough. I get the picture." Dad rested a hand on each of their shoulders to calm them down. "Goat Mountain isn't such a bad climb for boys or girls. If you want to climb it, you can all go. But you need someone who knows the way to take you up there. How about it, Casey? You want to take these climbers up Goat Mountain?" It wasn't exactly an order, but it really wasn't a question either.

Herding a bunch of eight- and nine-year-olds up Goat Mountain on a hot day was the last thing Casey wanted to do.

"Myca and Josie and I had other plans," he said, hoping his father would ask someone else.

"What kind of plans?" Dad asked.

"We were going rockhounding," Josie put in, when Casey couldn't think of anything to say. "Casey and Myca are teaching me how."

Dad grinned. "Well, then, a hike up Goat Mountain will fit right into your plans. And keep the peace," he added in a low voice only Casey could hear. "I'm counting on you, son."

Casey knew he couldn't refuse without giving away their real plans. He turned to Myca and Josie. "You want to come along?"

"Don't mind if I do," said Myca.

"It's a good place to hunt for rocks," said Josie.

"We'll take them, Dad," Casey agreed.

"Anybody else want to climb Goat Mountain?" Dad called.

Some of the younger cousins looked up at the high bluff

towering above the treetops beyond the road. Then they looked at each other and began to drift toward the beach.

"Greg and I want to go!" Toby called.

"It's going to be a real scorcher of a day," Casey warned. "Why don't we wait until later?"

"No! We want to go now!" Cindy and Butch both shouted at once.

"Let's take them and get it over with," said Josie. "We might even find a couple of good rocks."

"OK." Casey sighed. "We'll have to take along some water. The climb up there and back is going to take us a couple of hours, and there's not even a tiny spring up there."

"We don't want to come right back," Butch protested. "We want to stay up there and look around."

"Yeah, we want to look around," Buddy echoed. For once, Cindy and Megan agreed.

"I suppose we can stay for a little while," Casey said. At this rate they would never get a chance to put his plan into action. And who knew what would happen to Mr. B. before they got back.

"We'd better take along a lunch too," said Josie. "I'll go make up some sandwiches." She started for the house.

Casey glanced down at the twins' bare feet and the girls' sandals and thongs. "You all have to wear shoes and socks," he said. "Tennis shoes or hiking boots," he added when Cindy opened her mouth to argue. The kids all scattered to change.

"How long do you think it will be before we get over to Mr. B.'s?" asked Myca, when he and Casey were alone.

"About midnight, if we don't get these guys moving," said Casey in disgust. "I'm going to go fill the canteens."

"I've got to run home and call my mama and get my binoculars," said Myca. "I'll be back in no time." He trotted off across the yard.

The canteens were supposed to be in the storage cupboard on the back porch. But Casey couldn't find them. When he went into the kitchen to ask his mother about them, he found Josie filling one canteen at the sink.

"I'm filling this one with ice water, and I put punch for lunch in the other one," Josie said.

"We aren't going to be gone that long," said Casey, eyeing the mound of sandwiches on the counter. "You've got enough food there to feed all the relatives. How are we going to carry all that?"

Josie laughed. "That's only one sandwich apiece and a couple of cookies. We can put it all in your day pack."

"I'll go get it." Casey brought his pack from the coat rack on the back porch. He stuffed the sandwiches into the pack, then added a bag of cookies and a stack of paper cups. After fastening the flap, he stuck his arms though the straps of the pack.

"I'll bring the canteens," said Josie.

Toby and Greg and the twins were waiting in the shade of the red maple tree out front when Casey and Josie came around the house. A minute later, Cindy and Megan hurried out the front door in knee-high socks and tennis shoes.

"Is everybody ready to go?" Josie asked.

"We have to wait for Myca," said Casey. "He isn't back yet."

"Casey." His father motioned him to one side. "Remember, most of the kids haven't climbed Goat Mountain before," he said in a quiet voice. "You'd better take the easiest trail. And keep the kids away from the rock slide. We don't want any broken bones."

"We'll be careful, Dad."

Myca jumped the low fence next to the driveway and hurried to join them. "Sorry I was gone so long," he said. "I had to do a couple of chores for my mama and find my binoculars. I brought my rock bag."

Josie handed him a canteen. "Here, you get to carry this too."

"Guess I can handle that, if it means getting a drink when we get to the top." He slipped his head and arm through the canteen strap. "I'm ready, if you all are."

They were on their way down the driveway when Aunt Dee came running out of the house. "Cindy, you wait a minute," she called. Everybody turned and looked back. "You forgot to take your sunscreen lotion." Aunt Dee waved the bottle in the air as she hurried toward them. "You know how easily you burn. I want you to put some on before you go."

"Oh, Mom," Cindy moaned. She and Megan stopped to wait for Aunt Dee. The others walked slowly on down the road.

Hal was standing in front of Mr. B.'s mailbox sorting through the mail in his hands. He scowled when he came to a square, bright green envelope and started to open it. He heard them coming and quickly tucked the envelope between the folds of an advertisement.

"Where are you off to on a day as hot as this?" Hal leaned against Mr. Beckerman's mailbox and gave them his usual big, friendly smile. The boys all straggled to a stop.

"The kids want to climb Goat Mountain," said Casey.

"Goat Mountain?" Hal looked puzzled.

"It's right up there." Butch turned and pointed to the steep bluff jutting above the trees on the far side of the road.

"Yeah, right up there," said Buddy, nodding his head.

"Oh, that mountain." Hal gazed up at the bluff and laughed. "It's been so long I'd almost forgotten. For a minute I was expecting to see something a lot higher and more formidable. You kids still climbing the same old trails I climbed when I was a kid?"

"I guess so," said Casey. "We usually take the trail over there through the woods. But it's too steep for the little kids. So we're going on down the road to an easier trail. It takes longer, but it's safer for beginners."

"How is Mr. B. feeling today?" asked Myca.

Hal's smile faded. "I'm afraid there's no improvement," he said, stepping away from the mailbox. "Gramps still isn't ready for company. I'd better get back to the house. I don't like leaving him alone too long." He moved off down the driveway.

As Casey watched Hal hurry away, he had the funny feeling that it was Mr. B. who was in danger.

Chapter Nine

Spies on Goat Mountain

"Let's go," said Butch. "I'm not waiting for a bunch of girls."

"We're here," said Cindy, coming up behind them. She shoved the bottle of sunscreen lotion into Casey's pack. "I don't want to carry that all the way up Goat Mountain and back. Mom put so much on me, I'm not going to get sunburned."

The cousins straggled out along the road. Butch and Cindy took up their argument where they'd left off. As if it really mattered who reached the top first. Casey was tempted to take the first trail. It was a lot faster, and he wanted to get this trip over with and get on with his plan. But he kept going to the safer one. It was going to be a long, hot climb.

The patches of shade from the scattered pines and huge granite boulders were a welcome relief from the hot sun. Sweat had begun to trickle down Casey's back by the time they reached the cutoff to the trail. Casey took the lead. Myca and Josie let the little kids come next and fell in behind them.

"Hey, you missed the trail," Butch called. Casey looked back over his shoulder. Butch had already turned off and started to climb what looked like a trail, and Buddy was right behind him.

"That's not a trail. It's too steep to climb there," Casey called. "The trail is up ahead."

"This is not too steep for me," Butch bragged.

"It's not too steep," Buddy repeated.

It was a challenge that didn't go unnoticed by Cindy. The kids all shuffled to a stop and waited to see what the twins would do.

"That looks easy." Cindy turned to follow Butch and Buddy. "If they can climb it, so can we, can't we, Megan?"

From the look on Megan's face, she wasn't so sure, but she nodded. "We can do it."

Casey leaned his head back and looked up. Goat Mountain wasn't really a mountain at all. Just a steep bluff with trails leading to the top. And a great view of the lake and the surrounding area once you got there. He didn't doubt that Toby and maybe a couple of the others could make the steep climb. But if anything happened to one of them, he would be to blame. And Dad had said to take the easy trail, so he wasn't going to take any chances.

"It's too dangerous. We're taking the trail. Anybody who doesn't want to come with us has to go back." Casey expected an argument, but for once Butch turned around.

Cindy paused long enough to let Butch know she thought he was chicken before she followed along behind Casey again.

The next trail wasn't so steep and was far less dangerous. It started up at an easier angle and wound like a snake halfway to the top. Then it angled over and followed the edge of an ancient rock slide to the top. And not far from the end of the trail there was a small grove of pine trees. That would be a good place to eat their lunch.

"We're taking this trail," Casey called. He stopped and waited for the others to catch up.

"I think we should split up," said Josie. "One of us in the

lead, one in the middle, and one at the end in case anybody needs help."

"Good idea," said Casey. "Who wants to go first?"

"You keep the lead," said Myca. "I'll stay back here and help the stragglers along."

"I guess I'm stuck in the middle," said Josie.

Dust rose in a choking cloud as the kids scrambled up the trail like energetic monkeys. The group climbed for a while, then stopped to rest. Josie doled out drinks of water. We're already halfway up, Casey thought. Maybe we'll make it all the way to the top with no problems.

But when they reached the rock slide, he heard angry voices and looked back. Cindy and Megan had managed to get first in line behind him when they started to climb. Butch and Buddy had been satisfied to let them stay in the lead until the girls had begun to slow down.

"If you can't move any faster, get out of the way and let us pass," Butch yelled.

"Yeah, let us pass," Buddy repeated. Casey wondered if Buddy ever said anything that Butch hadn't said first.

Cindy stopped and flung her arms wide, blocking the trail. "You stay where you are, Butch Hilliard! This is our place in line."

"A snail could climb faster than you. Let us by," Butch insisted.

"Yeah, let us by," said Buddy.

"Cindy, stop arguing and get moving," Josie yelled. Cindy stood her ground. For a minute it looked like she was going to win. But instead of Butch and Buddy backing off, Butch left the trail. He climbed out onto the rock slide and started up to get around Cindy. Buddy was right behind him as usual. Casey sucked in a big breath. One misstep, and the whole rock slide could start moving.

"Butch! Buddy! Get off of there! It's too dangerous!"

Casey rushed back down the trail, slipping and sliding in his hurry to reach them.

Butch stepped onto a flat stone and looked up at Casey. "It's not . . ." Buddy stepped up beside him, and the stone began to teeter. Buddy's eyes widened in fear, and he grabbed hold of Butch.

"You want us to help?" Josie yelled, starting to climb.

"No, stay back!" Casey ordered. He worked his way carefully along the slide until he could reach Butch and Buddy. A shower of pebbles pattered down the rock slide like hail striking the roof. Casey knew what that meant.

"Please, God, don't let it come down yet," he whispered. There wasn't a second to lose. He reached out. "Take hold of my hands," Casey said quietly, fear coiling in his stomach. "Now jump!" He pulled hard at the same time. Both boys landed on firm ground.

"That wasn't danger . . ." Butch stopped talking when they heard the rumble and looked up.

For a split second, Casey froze. Then he leaped back. "Get down!" he shouted, shoving the twins away from the slide. Josie and Myca rushed to do the same. "Stay down!" Casey yelled above the deafening clatter. A huge boulder ricocheted off a slab of stone and rocketed past, followed by loose rocks bouncing and rattling down the slide.

Casey lay there until the sounds died away. He pushed himself up, spit the dirt out of his mouth, and got to his feet. He wiped his face with the back of his hand and looked at the others.

"You can get up now," he called. "Is everyone OK?"

Slowly the kids got to their feet, white faced and silent. Casey and Josie and Myca checked their elbows and knees and dusted them off.

"Everybody seems to be all right," said Myca. "Thanks to the good Lord for watching over us."

"He answered my prayer," said Casey, adding his own thanks.

"What happened?" Josie asked, sounding a little dazed.

"I'm not really sure," said Casey.

"Looks like it started up near the top," said Myca, pointing to the dark sides of the rocks that had been turned up during the slide.

"Well, whatever happened, it's over now," said Casey.

The excitement of the avalanche had put an end to the argument. Casey wasn't sure if Butch had won, or if Cindy and Megan had decided it was safer to let him and Buddy go first. Either way, the twins took the lead. They didn't waste any time finishing the climb. Up at the top, Casey and Myca looked over the rock slide. They found where the big boulder had been, but could see no reason for it to come loose.

"That makes it almost seem like it was pried loose," said Josie.

"Why would anybody do that?" Casey didn't want to think about it. He led the way to the pine grove and shrugged off his pack. The fragrant, warm smell of the pines hung in the hot, dusty air.

"Anybody thirsty?" Josie asked, pulling off her canteen. Everybody crowded around as Casey got out the paper cups. The ice had melted, but there was still enough water for one more drink apiece. The kids gulped it down and held out their cups for more.

"How about some lunch?" asked Josie. "We brought sandwiches and cookies. There's punch too." She started pulling sandwiches out of Casey's pack and passing them around. The kids settled down in the shade to eat. Casey passed out the cookies while Myca filled their cups.

Josie took the last three sandwiches out of the pack and dropped it in the shade beside a big granite boulder. "All that climbing made me hungry," she said, handing Casey and Myca each a sandwich before she sat down with her back to a tree.

They ate quickly, dividing the last of the cookies and punch evenly among the kids. When they were finished, Butch wanted to go exploring.

Toby jumped to his feet. "I've been up here lots of times," he said importantly. "Come on, I'll show you around." They all got up and trailed after him. Toby answered their questions as he led them off through the dried grass and stubby sagebrush. Casey didn't bother to follow them. They couldn't go far.

"Let's go take a look at the lake," said Myca. He took his binoculars out of the case as they walked toward the edge of the bluff. "I've been wanting to try these out from up here."

The climb up Goat Mountain had been a long one. But the distance was mostly up. They could look down at the houses and out over the lake.

Myca adjusted the binoculars and grinned. "There's my house! And yours, Casey. I can see your mama sitting out on the patio talking to your aunts. She's fanning herself with the newspaper."

"Can you really see all that?" Josie asked in disbelief.

"Just like I was standing in the yard." Myca handed her the binoculars. Josie fiddled with the adjustment knob for a minute, then panned the side of the lake. "You can!" she cried. "These are really powerful."

"Let me have a look," said Casey. Josie gave him the binoculars. Casey scanned his yard, then moved on across the hedge to Mr. Beckerman's and stopped. "There are two strange men down there in Mr. B.'s yard."

Myca took the binoculars. "Those are the antique dealers I was telling you about," he said. "They must have mistaken Mr. B.'s house for the one they're looking for. Now they're leaving."

"Let me see." Josie grabbed the binoculars. "They're not leaving. Hal just came running up the driveway. He's shaking hands with them. Now he's taking them into the house."

"We'd better get down there and find out what's going on." Casey turned to leave. "I'll find the kids. You get our stuff."

"By the time we get the kids back down the trail, those men will most likely be gone," said Myca.

"I guess you're right. But we can keep an eye on Mr. B.'s house. We might find out what Hal is up to," said Casey. They took turns, passing the binoculars back and forth.

Finally Josie glanced at her watch. "We've been here for an hour. I'm ready to go home. How about you?"

"I've been ready since we got here." Casey strode back to the grove of pine trees and picked up his pack. "Toby, it's time to go," he yelled.

"I'm not ready to go yet," Butch argued, his face red and damp.

"I thought you said we could stay a while," Cindy complained.

"We have stayed a while. Now it's time to go back to the lake for a swim," said Josie, smiling brightly. "Won't that feel great!"

Butch and Cindy eyed each other, waiting to see who was going to give in first.

It was Buddy who spoke first. "Yeah, great," he said, looking hot and dusty. "I want to go for a swim."

"Me too," said Megan. Together they headed for the trail.

For a minute Butch just stared, his mouth hanging open in shocked surprise. Then he sprinted after them, yelling, "Hey, Buddy, wait for me!"

Cindy was only a step behind him.

Chapter Ten

Figuring Out a Plan

It took a lot less time to hike down from Goat Mountain than it had to climb it. When they reached the end of the trail, Casey led the group to a shortcut through the sun-dried grass and tall weeds. Every step flushed grasshoppers from their hiding places. They reached the road and turned toward home, trudging along, looking hot and tired. For once, Butch and Cindy didn't have anything to say. But when the house came into view, everyone moved a little faster.

"Last one in the lake is a toad!" Greg yelled. The kids all found enough energy to sprint up the driveway. Casey and Josie and Myca stopped in the shade of the red maple to catch their breath.

"I wish we knew if those antique dealers are still over at Mr. B.'s," said Casey.

"I looked down his driveway as we came past, but I couldn't see their car," said Josie.

"We have to go over there and find out what's happening," said Casey. "I've got this funny feeling about Mr. B."

"How're we going to go snooping around over there without Hal figuring out what we're up to?" Myca asked.

"Easy," said Casey, lowering his voice. "You go over there and tell Hal you want your rock. You know, the one Mr. B.

was cutting for you the day Hal came. Tell him Mr. B. forgot to give it back to you in all the excitement. Try to get him to go out to the workshop with you. Then while you're keeping him busy, Josie and I will slip into the house and see what's happened to Mr. B."

"That's a good plan," said Myca. "But what if Hal won't go along with me to the workshop? What do we do then?"

"You just have to talk him into it," said Casey. "You'll think of something."

"What if we can't get into the house?" asked Josie.

"Will you guys stop saying 'what if'!" Casey demanded through tight teeth. "We'll worry about all that when we get to it."

"All right," Josie agreed. "But we can't go over there looking like this. We're all hot and sweaty and covered with dust."

"Casey! Casey, where are you?" his mother shouted. "I want to talk to you this minute."

"Your mother sounds really upset," said Myca.

"Something must be wrong," said Josie.

"There hasn't been time for anything to go wrong," said Casey. "We just got back. Nobody can get into trouble that fast. Come on, we'd better go find out what it's all about."

By the time they reached the house, some of the kids had rushed off to change into their swimsuits. Toby and Greg and Megan and Buddy were on their way down to the lake under the watchful eye of Aunt Libby. But Butch and Cindy were still dressed in their hiking clothes. They were both talking to Mom and Aunt Dee and Aunt Estelle.

"I should have known it would be those two." Casey sighed.

"What happened on your hike?" his mother asked before Casey and Josie and Myca got across the patio.

"Butch said he and Buddy almost got caught in a rock slide," Aunt Estelle accused. "They might have been killed."

Casey noticed that Butch didn't say what they were doing on the rock slide. "Nobody got hurt," said Casey. "A big rock came down from up above and brought a bunch of smaller rocks with it."

They finally got the rock slide explained to everybody's satisfaction. Butch and Cindy rushed off to change.

"After all that, I could sure use a swim myself," said Myca.

"Me too," Josie agreed. "How about you, Casey?"

The shimmering water of the lake did look cool and inviting, but Casey shook his head. "We have to find out what's going on over at Mr. B's."

"We can do both," said Josie. "From the beach, we can see if there is a car parked in front of Mr. B.'s garage."

"And we get a chance to cool off too," said Myca, pushing his cap back and wiping his dripping forehead on his arm.

It was an offer Casey couldn't refuse. "OK, but just for a quick swim."

"I'll be back as soon as I change into my swim trunks," said Myca. "Meet you at the lake."

Casey and Josie went into the house to change. By the time Myca returned, they were waiting with their towels draped across their shoulders. They raced across the hot sand and plunged into the lake. The water felt good as Casey swam a few strokes under the surface and came up to suck in a breath of air. He paddled over to where Josie and Myca were splashing around, up to their shoulders.

"This feels great," Myca said, rolling over to float on his back.

"Yeah," Josie agreed, swimming closer to Mr. B's buoy line.

"Can you see anything?" Casey whispered.

Slowly Josie turned and looked up past the beach to Mr. B.'s yard. "There's a car parked behind Hal's old heap," she said in a low voice. "The antique dealers must still be there."

They took turns swimming over the line, keeping an eye on the car.

Finally Josie got tired. "You want to swim out to the float?" she asked. "We can see Mr. B's yard from there too."

Casey glanced in that direction. Toby and Greg and the twins were there with Cindy and Megan and Aunt Libby. "No, there are too many people out there."

They got out of the water and sat on the beach for a while. When they went back into the lake, they worked their way to the buoy line again.

"I can't believe they're still there," Josie said, when she got back to Casey and Myca. They must be checking out every piece of furniture in the whole house."

"We have to get over there and see what's happening," said Casey, casting a dark look in the direction of Mr. B.'s house.

"We just can't go barging in," said Josie. "We'll have to wait until those men are gone."

Aunt Libby and all the kids came in from the float. "Isn't the water wonderful?" Aunt Libby called. She spread out her towel in the sand and sat down. "Now I'm going to soak up some sun." The kids started splashing around in the shallow water and building sand castles on the beach.

"Let's go out to the float now," Josie said in a low voice. "We can watch better from there."

They took turns diving off the board for a while, then flopped down on the float to warm themselves in the sun and keep an eye on the car in Mr. B.'s yard. Aunt Libby and the kids had gone up to the house before Casey saw the two men drive away.

"There they go! Now is our chance." Casey leaped to his feet.

"Wait for us," Myca called. They swam back to shore and hurried up the lawn to the patio.

"I'll be back as soon as I change," said Myca.

Casey nodded. "We'll take the shortcut through the hedge." He turned to Josie and said, "Meet us out in front when you're ready."

Casey was the first one there. He had only been waiting a couple of minutes in the shade of the big rhododendron bush when Myca came around the corner of the house.

"Where's Josie?" Myca asked.

"Not here yet," Casey grumbled impatiently.

Josie's red hair was still wet when she finally slipped out the front door. "Sorry it took me so long," she said. "Aunt Dee insisted on hearing about the rock slide again. And why we didn't make Cindy use her sunscreen lotion. I had to explain everything all over again."

"I hope you told her it was nobody's fault," said Casey.

"I told her. And that we were right there with them when it happened."

"That rock slide was too close for me," said Myca.

"Forget about all that," said Casey. "We've got more important things to think about."

"Are you sure this is going to work?" Josie asked.

"Of course I'm sure. It's too simple not to work. Myca goes up to the house and tells Hal he wants his rock back. Then he gets Hal to go out to the workshop with him to get it. And while they're gone, you and I slip into the house and see Mr. B."

"How come I have to be the one?" said Myca, rubbing his hands together, the way he always did when he got nervous.

"Because it's your rock, and Hal knows it," said Casey.

"But what if Hal won't come out of the house?" Myca kept rubbing his hands together. "What do I do then?"

"You'll think of something," Casey assured him. "Come on, let's go." He moved across the lawn and slipped through the hole in the hedge. He took a quick look around. "All clear," he whispered. Josie and Myca followed him through the hole.

"Stay out of sight until we get close to the house," said Casey. They worked their way from bush to bush and tree to tree until they reached the big evergreen bush near the porch. From there they could hear everything on the porch.

"OK, Myca, go knock on the door," Casey whispered. "And try to sound convincing when you tell Hal you need to get your rock back."

Myca sucked in a big, shaky breath, then another one, like he was pumping up his courage. "Wish me luck," he whispered. Stepping away from the bush, he strode up onto the porch and disappeared in the deep shadows. Then the brass knocker tapped on Mr. B.'s door.

Casey held his breath until they heard the door open and Hal say, "Oh, it's you. I told you kids, Gramps isn't himself yet."

"I didn't come to see Mr. B." Myca talked fast, as if Hal were shutting the door in his face. "I came to get my rock. The one Mr. B. cut for me the day you came. It's out in the workshop."

"Come back later when Gramps is better," Hal told him. "I'm busy right now, so go on home."

"I can't wait, I need it right away," Myca insisted. "I met this kid—he's a rockhound too. And he wants to trade me a mighty fine piece of geode for my rock. He's leaving in the morning, so I have to have it."

"Go out to the workshop and get it." Hal started to close the door.

"Mr. B. doesn't allow us in the workshop alone. You have to come with me," Myca pleaded.

"Oh, for . . . All right! All right!" Hal stepped onto the porch and slammed the door behind him. "I'll go with you to get your rock, but you'd better not take all day; I've got things to do," Hal warned. They left the porch and started down the white gravel path to the workshop.

The minute they were out of sight, Josie moved away

from the bush. "That wasn't a very good hiding place," she whispered, rubbing her bare arms where the prickly bush had touched her skin.

"Next time we'll pick a better one," said Casey, rubbing his arms too. "We haven't got much time. Myca might not be able to keep him away for long. And we have to find Mr. B." They hurried toward the house.

Chapter Eleven

In Search of Mr. B.

Casey rushed up onto the porch and reached for the door. His hand was slippery with sweat as he turned the knob. "It's not locked."

"What are we going to do if Hal comes back and catches us?" Josie whispered, crowding close behind him.

"Worry about that later. Right now we have to find Mr. B. and make sure he's OK." Casey shoved the door open and peeked inside. It took a few seconds to adjust his eyes to the dimness of the hall.

"Why is it so dark in here? Josie whispered.

"Hal must have all the drapes closed. That's not a good sign. Mr. B. always has them open this time of day." Casey closed the door softly.

"Look." Josie grabbed Casey's arm and pointed to the bright yellow sticker on the grandfather clock standing near the stairway. They crept down the hall, peeking into the dimly lighted living room as they passed. Josie stepped into the room and looked around. "Those stickers are on half the furniture in here too," she said.

Casey bent close to the sticker on the curio cabinet. "It says, 'S&E Antiques.' This must be the furniture those men want to buy. Come on, we haven't got time for this if we're gonna find Mr. B."

They made a quick search of the downstairs rooms without success. Casey hurried back to the staircase in the front hall and took the stairs two at a time. Josie rushed after him. At the top of the stairs the upstairs hall led off in both directions.

"Which room is Mr. B.'s?" Josie asked.

"The master bedroom there at the end of the hall." They crept down the hall, and Casey opened the door. "Mr. B.? You in here?" The room was empty.

"Whoever made the bed didn't do a very good job," said Josie. "And look, there are yellow stickers on the furniture in here too."

"Mr. B. has to be here somewhere," said Casey. "Let's search the rest of the rooms. You take the right side of the hall, and I'll take the left. Don't yell if you find Mr. B. Just come and get me. I'll do the same."

"OK." Josie rushed off down the hall, opening doors. It took them less than three minutes to search the six bedrooms and the bathroom. Mr. B. wasn't in any of them.

"Where can he be?" Josie said as they met at the top of the stairs.

"He has to be here somewhere." Casey raked his hand through his hair and tried not to think about what might be in the attic or the basement. Suddenly he said, "Wait a minute! I think I've got it!"

"We haven't got very many minutes left." Josie's voice trembled a little. "Hal might be back any second. We have to get out of here."

"There's one place we haven't looked." Casey grabbed Josie by the arm and rushed down the hall.

"In a closet?" Josie stared in disbelief as he opened a small door.

Casey opened the door wider to show a narrow flight of stairs. "It leads to the kitchen downstairs. Come on." He flipped a light switch, and a feeble light came on at the foot of the stairs. Josie started down. Casey closed the door behind them. The steep, narrow stairway was thick with dust.

"Faaa! Patooey!" Josie kept spitting and scrubbing the back of her hand across her mouth.

"What's the matter?" Casey remembered to keep his voice down.

"Cobwebs!" Josie rubbed her hands across her face and waved her arms in front of her. "This place is full of them."

"These stairs haven't been used for a long time." As if to prove it, the light bulb burned out.

"Caseeeey, I'm scared." Josie's voice quavered. "There are spiders in here. And I can't see."

"Don't think about 'em. Keep going. It's not very far to the bottom." Casey knew just how she felt. He didn't like spiders either. His heart was thumping hard against his ribs. "Put your hands out and touch the walls on each side to guide you," he whispered, as he did the same and hoped he wouldn't touch anything else.

Only the gasps of their quick breathing and the soft thud of their tennis shoes filled the small, narrow space. The steps seemed to go on forever.

"I found the door!" Josie fumbled for the knob. A second later a crack of light appeared. Then they were stumbling out into the bright, sunny kitchen.

Casey blinked in the sudden light, then headed across the floor. "This used to be the hired girl's room," he said, opening a white painted door. "It's the only one we haven't searched."

"Casey! I heard the front door close!" Josie's fingers dug into his arm as she looked over her shoulder at the swinging door that led to the hall. "We have to get out of here!"

"Not before I see what's in here." Casey shoved the door open. Mr. B. was stretched out on the narrow bed in his bathrobe. The stubble of whiskers on his face made him look even more pale and drawn. His white hair was a matted tangle. It looked as if it hadn't been combed for days.

"Mr. B.?" Casey whispered in an urgent voice. "Mr. B., can you hear me?" He took a step toward the bed. The old man's eyes were closed.

"He's coming, Casey!" Josie's voice was edged with panic.

For a split second, Casey hesitated. He was so close. But if they got caught, they couldn't help Mr. B. "We'll be back, I promise," he whispered to the still form on the bed. Then Casey hurried back into the kitchen and closed the door softly.

He grabbed Josie by the hand. "This way," he whispered. They made it out the kitchen door as the swinging door opened. Casey dragged Josie behind a clump of bushes and waited until he was sure Hal hadn't followed them.

"That was close!" Josie whispered, holding a hand over her heart. "I thought Hal was going to catch us."

Casey pushed the branches aside and peeked out. Hal was nowhere in sight. "If we had just found Mr. B. a couple of minutes sooner, we'd know if he's all right."

"Mr. B. was asleep. I could hear him breathing, so he's all right," said Josie.

"If he's all right, what was he doing in that room instead of his own bedroom? I don't like this, Josie. Something weird is going on." Casey peeked out again. "Let's go find Myca." They moved quietly away from the house and hurried toward the hole in the hedge.

Myca stepped out from behind the big quince bush and breathed a sigh of relief. "I thought Hal gotcha for sure. Did you find Mr. B.?"

"We found him," said Casey. "But Hal came back before we had a chance to talk to him. I wish you could have kept him away just a little longer."

"A little longer!" Myca threw his hands up. "I had to do

some fast and fancy talking to keep Hal away as long as I did. He wasn't too sociable, I can tell you. He was wanting to get back to the house, and he didn't take too kindly to my going on about Mr. B. being such a great rockhound. Or asking questions about that rock collection of his. He kept after me to get my rock and get out of there."

"You kept him away a lot longer than I could have," said Josie.

"If we'd found Mr. B. right away, we would have had plenty of time."

"Where is Hal now?" asked Myca.

"He was in the house when we got out the back door," said Casey. "I think he's still there. Why?"

"Come on, I want to show you something," said Myca.

They moved toward the workshop, careful to keep a screen of shrubs and bushes between themselves and the house.

"Is this important?" Casey asked. "I don't want to get caught hanging around here. We have to help Mr. B., and we can't if we get grounded."

"It's important," said Myca. "And it's mighty strange too. For a rockhound, Hal sure doesn't know much about rocks. When we got to the workshop, I told him I was looking for the geode Mr. B. had just cut for me. Hal picked up a piece of jasper Mr. B. had cut for one of his craft projects and tried to give it to me."

"Are you serious?" said Josie. "Even I know the difference between a geode and jasper, and I'm just a beginner."

Before they stepped out from behind the bushes near the workshop, they all took a look around. "The coast is clear over here," Myca whispered.

"Here too," said Josie in a low voice.

"Don't waste any time getting inside," said Casey. They dashed across the exposed driveway in front of the garage and ducked into the workshop.

"Now, what do you want to show us?" Casey asked.

"It's not something you would notice right off," said Myca. "I stumbled onto it by accident when I knocked a couple of rocks off Mr. B.'s bench." Myca motioned them across the room to the shelves that held Mr. B.'s rock displays. "If you look closely, you'll see that some of Mr. B.'s best rocks are missing."

Casey walked quickly up and down the rows of shelves. "Hey, they are missing. I wonder what happened to them?"

"That's what I wanted to show you. Look over here." Myca crossed the room to the large workbench where Mr. B. kept his finished craft work. Myca bent down and lifted the top of one of the wooden crates under the table. "The rocks are all packed up in these crates. And look at this." He closed the lid of the crate and pointed to a newly addressed shipping label. "That's the rock shop Mr. B. sells rocks to sometimes."

"What so strange about that?" asked Josie.

Casey kneeled down and sorted through the rocks in the crate. "Look, here's the thunderegg Mr. B. was going to make into his next pair of bookends." Casey picked it up. "He's already cut it in two. Why would he sell it like this when he gets such a good price for his bookends? It doesn't make sense."

"I don't think Mr. B. had anything to do with it," said Myca. "Remember all of the finished work Mr. B. had crated up to take to the gift shops at Lloyd Center in Portland? They're not here anymore. Mr. B. most likely took Hal along when he went to deliver them."

"You mean to introduce Hal to the people he knows in the shops? What difference would that make?" Josie asked.

"I think it gave Hal some notions about rocks," Myca said, digging a paper out from under a pile of Mr. B.'s craft-design sketches. "This was lying on the workbench when we came in a while ago. Hal tried to hide it, but I got a peek at it first."

"What is it?" asked Josie, looking over Myca's shoulder to see.

"A list of rocks the rock shop wants and what they are willing to pay," said Myca. "The owner of the rock shop gives Mr. B. one every time he goes in there."

Casey reached over and took the list. He looked it over and nodded. "The rocks that are missing from the shelves are checked off on this list."

"But I thought you said Hal didn't know anything about rocks," said Josie. "How do you know it wasn't Mr. B. who crated them up?"

"Easy as pie," said Myca. "Mr. B. has all of the rocks labeled. All Hal had to do was go along and pick out the right ones. But look here," he pointed to the list, "three of these rocks are right over there on that bench in plain sight. Only Hal didn't know that. 'Cause those rocks don't have labels."

Casey slammed down the rock he was holding. "Hal isn't going to get away with robbing Mr. B. I'm going to tell Dad what's been going on over here. He'll know what to do." Casey strode out the door and headed for the hedge, not caring if Hal saw him or not.

Chapter Twelve

To Stop a Thief

They slipped back through the hedge and went around the house to the patio. Casey was all ready to blurt out the whole story, even if he did get grounded. But Dad and Casey's aunts and uncles and all the cousins were playing football. There was a lot of laughing and shouting and screaming going on. It looked like fun and not something he could interrupt without having to tell everybody the whole story. For a minute, Casey wished they were right in the middle of the game having fun too.

"What are we going to do now?" asked Myca.

"Maybe we should tell Aunt Rose instead," said Josie.

Casey nodded. "We have to tell somebody and right away. Hal is getting ready to sell Mr. B.'s furniture and a lot of other stuff in the house. And who knows what awful thing he's going to do to Mr. B.? We have to stop him. But this time try to stay calm when we talk to Mom."

They found her in the kitchen, mixing up a huge green salad.

Mom added green pepper she'd been chopping to the salad and smiled at them. "Three helpers, just what I need." She pointed to a big basket of fresh corn. "How about pulling the husks off that corn for me?" she asked, reaching for a tomato.

"We will, Mom, but first we have to talk to you," said Casey.

His mother turned to look at them. "What happened? From the look on your faces, it must be pretty serious." She put the tomato and her knife down and gave them her full attention. "Tell me what's wrong."

"It's Mr. B.," said Casey. "We were just over there and . . ."

"Casey," Mom interrupted, "you were told not to bother Mr. Beckerman while his grandson is here."

"I know, Mom, but we were really worried about him. We haven't seen Mr. B. since the day we found him staggering around in his yard mumbling to himself. And we haven't talked to him since Hal came."

"There have been some weird things going on over there," said Josie. "We wanted to talk to Mr. B. and make sure he's all right."

"What kind of weird things?" Rose Hilliard asked, her forehead puckering into a frown.

"Antique dealers, for one thing," said Myca. He told her what he'd overheard at the restaurant. "Today we saw them at Mr. B.'s. Hal invited them in, and they spent a mighty long time over there."

"And we saw yellow stickers with the name 'S&E Antiques' on a lot of the furniture when we were in the house a while ago," said Josie.

"That's right." Casey nodded in agreement. "And there was Mr. Sidel too. Remember him, Mom? He's the man who has been trying to buy Mr. B.'s property."

"I remember," Mom said, folding her arms and leaning against the counter. "Go on."

"Mr. Sidel has been over there too," said Casey. "We saw him shake hands with Hal. Then Hal signed some papers."

"But we didn't see Mr. B. at all," said Myca. "We got to wondering if he was all right. So we went over there to see for ourselves."

Mom pressed her lips together tight. Casey knew that look. But all she said was, "Go on. What happened then?"

Casey looked at Josie and Myca. "We better tell her everything."

"Yes, that's a very good idea," his mother said. "If you did something wrong, I want to know about it now."

"We were afraid Hal wouldn't let us see Mr. B.," said Casey, "so we sort of tricked him."

"I got Hal to go out to the workshop with me," Myca explained, "while Casey and Josie slipped into the house to see Mr. B."

"Casey, I can't believe you three did such a thing. Sneaking into Mr. Beckerman's house." Mom shook her head. "You know better."

"Mom, we had to. There really is something wrong," Casey insisted. "We couldn't even find Mr. B. at first. We looked all over the house. We finally found him in that little room off the kitchen, the one that Mr. B. calls the hired girl's room."

"What did Mr. Beckerman say about your barging in?" Mom asked.

"He didn't say anything," Casey answered. "Mr. B. was lying on the bed asleep or unconscious. He looked awful, Mom. His hair was all wild, and he hasn't shaved for days. We didn't have time to find out if he was all right. You have to help him, Mom."

It was a long minute before his mother spoke. She rubbed her hand across her hair and said, "I find all of this very hard to believe, but if what you say is true, it needs looking into." She moved over to the sink and washed her hands. "You three get started on that corn," she said. "I'm going over to have a little chat with Hal and Mr. Beckerman. I'll be right back."

"We did it!" Casey gave, first Myca, then Josie, a high-five before they jumped around the room, grinning. "We really did it! Now Mr. B.'s stuff will be saved, and so will he."

Josie stopped bouncing around and got serious again. "What if Hal doesn't let Aunt Rose in? What if he closes the door in her face?"

"Don't worry about that," said Casey. "If anybody can find out what's going on over there, it's Mom. And she won't give up until she gets to talk to Mr. B. in person."

It was a relief to know Mom had taken over, and he didn't have to worry about Mr. B. anymore. Casey wanted to go outside and flop on the grass. Somewhere in the shade, so he could stare up at the sky and forget there were ever any problems.

"We'd better get the corn husked before Aunt Rose comes back," said Josie. "We did promise to do it for her."

"I almost forgot about that," said Myca. "You want to do it in here or take the corn outside?"

"Outside," said Casey. He felt too good to be cooped up in the house. He grabbed one handle of the basket. Myca grabbed the other side.

"I'll get a pan for the corn," said Josie, and she turned to open the cupboard door. Casey and Myca carried the basket outside. They stopped at the bottom of the porch steps and looked for a place to work.

"There's a good spot." Josie walked past them to the shady side of the maple tree. The boys set the basket down and sat down cross-legged beside it. They each took an ear of corn and tore away the husks. Casey kept looking toward the driveway after he dropped each ear into the pan. By the time the basket was half-empty, Josie and Myca were looking too, but Rose Hilliard still hadn't come back.

"I wonder what's taking Mom so long," said Casey. "She should have been back by now."

"What if something happened to her?" The half-finished ear of corn dropped from Josie's hand unnoticed as she started to get up.

"Wait a few more minutes," said Casey. "If she isn't back by the time we finish the corn, we'll tell Dad where she is and have him go over there with us."

Chapter Thirteen

Smells Like a Polecat to Me

They worked quickly, ripping away the green husks and pulling off the strands of corn silk. There were five more ears of corn in the bottom of the basket. Casey had picked one up when he saw his mother come around the corner of the house.

"Mom!" Casey dropped the ear of corn and jumped to his feet. "What took you so long?"

"I've just had a long talk with Hal." Mom's face looked almost grim. Josie and Myca were on their feet too, moving closer to her, waiting to hear the news. But Rose Hilliard just stood there with a far-off look in her eyes.

"Mom, what happened? Is Mr. B. all right?" Casey took hold of his mother's arm and shook her a little, trying to bring her back from wherever her thoughts had taken her.

She blinked, then turned her gaze on the three of them. "I have a lot to tell all of you," she said. "Let's go over there and sit down."

She didn't say any more until they were all settled at the picnic table, waiting expectantly. Mom clasped her hands together and took a big breath, then let it out slowly.

"Everything you told me is true," she said in a quiet voice. "Mr. Sidel was over there talking to Hal about buying the house. And the men from the antique shop were there

97

picking out the pieces of furniture and things they want to buy."

"See, we were right!" Casey cried triumphantly. "He was trying to steal Mr. B.'s stuff."

"No, that's where you're wrong," his mother said, shaking her head.

"Mom, you're supposed to be helping Mr. B., not agreeing with Hal," Casey argued.

She reached out and put her hand over Casey's. "There is much more to it than you know."

"But we know Mr. B. would never agree to sell his things," Josie insisted.

"And Hal's trying to sell off some of Mr. B.'s best rocks," Myca added. "I found 'em all boxed up in the workshop."

"Listen to me, all of you," Mom said. "I hate to tell you this, because I know how much you like Mr. Beckerman. But he is a very sick man and has been for some time. That's why Mr. Beckerman asked Hal to come and help take care of him."

"What kind of help is that?" Josie cried.

"What's wrong with Mr. B.?" asked Myca.

"It's called Alzheimer's disease," Rose Hilliard said. "Something that comes on gradually. One minute a person is perfectly normal, and the next they turn into a complete stranger. As the disease progresses, they lose touch with reality and fail to recognize the people closest to them. Even their loved ones. And they can become violent. That's what is happening to Mr. Beckerman."

"Myca and I have spent a lot of time with Mr. B., and he's never acted like that," Casey insisted.

"You haven't been spending a lot of time with him lately," his mother reminded him.

"Well, no," Casey admitted. "But that's because Mr. B. has been really busy with his crafts. He was all set to take us rockhounding when Hal showed up."

"I don't believe Mr. B. wrote and ask Hal to come," said Josie. "He was surprised to see Hal when he showed up."

"Hal told me when Mr. Beckerman found out from the doctor what was wrong with him, he wrote and asked for Hal's help. By the time Hal arrived, Mr. Beckerman had forgotten he was coming. It's part of the disease," Mom explained. "Hal loves his grandfather."

"If Hal loves Mr. B. so much, why is he trying to sell all his stuff?" asked Casey.

"Hal isn't doing it because he wants to," his mother explained. "When Hal first arrived, Mr. Beckerman gave him what's called power of attorney. That means Hal can take care of all Mr. Beckerman's business matters, like selling his house and his furniture. Even his rocks," she said, looking at Myca. "And that is what Hal is doing. Mr. Beckerman is too sick to take care of his affairs himself. So Hal is doing it for him."

"But that's not fair!" Casey shouted. "Mr. B. loves that house. He told Mr. Sidel a hundred times he'd never sell. If Hal really cares about Mr. B., he wouldn't sell it either."

"I'm afraid Hal doesn't have a choice," his mother said in a soft voice. "Hal can't stay here and take care of his grandfather. In a few days he has to go back East. Before he leaves, Hal wants to get his grandfather settled in a nursing home, where he will be well cared for."

"Mr. B. is going to live in a nursing home?" Casey cried.

"It's for the best," Mom said. "Nursing homes are very expensive. Hal must sell Mr. Beckerman's property to pay for his care. That's why he accepted Mr. Sidel's offer so quickly. And why he let the antique dealers go through the house and have first choice of the best pieces of furniture. It isn't something Hal wants to do. It's something he has to do."

Myca picked at a tiny sliver of loose wood on the edge of the picnic table. "When is Mr. B. going away?"

Mom rubbed her fingers over her forehead. "Let me see." She thought for a minute. "Hal has arranged to have the rest of Mr. Beckerman's things auctioned off the day after tomorrow. An estate sale, he called it."

Casey jumped up from the table. "Hal's going to sell everything?"

"It's the easiest and quickest way," his mother explained. "Hal said something about moving Mr. Beckerman to Shady Pines before the auction starts so he won't be upset."

"Does that mean we'll never see Mr. B. again?" Casey swallowed hard at the lump in his throat.

"Of course not." His mother patted his hand. "You can visit Mr. Beckerman in the nursing home once he gets settled."

"I want to go over and see him." Josie got to her feet.

"I'm afraid there is no point in going over there now," said Mom, standing up and putting her arm around her niece. "I peeked in on Mr. Beckerman while I was there. He was asleep in the back room. Hal said he'd been like that most of the day."

"Maybe Mr. B. will be better tomorrow," said Myca. He unfolded his long legs from under the picnic table.

"If he is, will Hal let us see him then? We'd like to see Mr. B. before he goes away," Casey said.

"I'm not sure Mr. Beckerman will be up to it. But I'm glad you all understand Hal is doing what's best for his grandfather. Losing a good friend is hard, but these things happen in life. And there is nothing we can do to change it," Mom said.

"Thanks for finding out about Mr. B. for us, Mom."

Just then the football game broke up, and everybody started toward the patio, still laughing and out of breath.

"What have you got to feed a hungry crowd?" Dad yelled. "We've worked up a real appetite."

"Oh, I forgot all about dinner! Is the corn ready?" Mom

turned and saw the pan filled with the husked ears. "Thanks, kids."

"There are a few more ears to husk," said Josie.

"When you're finished, bring them in." Mom scooped up the pan of corn and started up the porch steps. "Dinner will be ready in a few minutes," she called to Dad, and hurried into the house.

"Do you believe Mr. B. really wants Hal to sell his house?" asked Myca as they finished husking the last ears of corn.

"No way. I won't believe it until I hear it from Mr. B. himself," Casey vowed.

"Me either," Josie agreed. "There are too many weird things happening."

"It all smells like a polecat to me," said Myca. "If Mr. B. has been sick for a long time with that forgetting disease, how come he never forgot anything when we were with him?"

"That's a good question." Casey reached for the last ear of corn and peeled the husks back. "Why didn't anyone else notice that there was something wrong before now? Why did it start after Hal got here?"

"We'll never find the answers to those questions before it's too late," said Josie. "Mr. B. will be gone the day after tomorrow."

Chapter Fourteen

The Green Envelope

Josie gathered up the ears of corn. "I'll take these in to Aunt Rose. You guys pick up the corn silk and husks and put them in the basket. I'll be back in a minute."

"After we finish up here, I gotta go," said Myca.

"You can stay for dinner," said Casey. "Mama won't mind."

Myca shook his head. "Got orders from my mother. This morning, she told me I was to come have dinner at the restaurant with her and Daddy tonight."

"You could call her and ask," Casey suggested.

"No, sir. The special on the menu tonight is my favorite." Myca grinned. "Cajun beans and rice." He patted his lean stomach. "Nobody can make Cajun beans like my daddy. Best in the whole world."

Casey grinned too. "I know they are. I guess you have to go, then. Josie and I will try to figure out a way to say goodbye to Mr. B. before Hal sends him off to that nursing home."

Myca picked up the last of the cornhusks and tossed them into the basket. "I'll be back before dark. And I'll try to come up with an idea or two on the way home." Myca checked to make sure he had his key and hopped on his bike. "See you later."

Josie and Casey couldn't find a place to talk over ideas

without some of the cousins listening in until dinner was over. After the picnic table had been cleared and the paper plates and cups picked up from the patio, Casey went looking for Josie. There were still too many kids running around—too many adults lounging in the patio chairs.

Casey found Josie settling another argument.

"Remember, no more fighting," Josie said, shaking her finger at Butch and Cindy. "Why don't you get the other kids together and make up teams? Then you can all play with the basketball."

"Forget that!" said Cindy. "He can have the old ball." She threw the basketball at Butch and stalked off.

Josie shrugged and made a what-can-you-do face. "You win some, you lose some," she said.

"Let's take a walk down by the lake so we can talk," said Casey.

They ambled along the path to the beach without saying anything. The lake was as smooth as glass. Later, Casey knew, the moon would be there reflected on the surface, like a face in a mirror.

A warm, soft breeze brought the fragrant smell from the small grove of pines Mr. B. had left near the lake to attract the squirrels and chipmunks. It was always fun to listen to them scold and chatter when you got too close. And even more fun to watch when Mr. B. tossed food in the grass for them. Casey always had to cover his mouth with his hand to keep from laughing out loud when the squirrels scampered down from the trees and grabbed a tidbit in their front paws. The chipmunks kept a bright eye turned in your direction while they stuffed the food in their cheeks. Then with a flick of their tails, they would be gone.

Gone. The word sent a shiver down Casey's spine. Without Mr. B., it would all be gone. The house, the pine grove, the huge oak trees, the workshop, and the rocks. Everything would be cleared away. In its place, Mr. Sidel planned to put four or five houses with postage stamp–sized yards and a common access path to the beach. It was going to be terrible.

Josie shoved her hands into the pockets of her walking shorts and gazed out over the water. "I'm really going to miss Mr. B."

"I wish Hal had never come here." Casey kicked out in sudden anger, sending a shower of sand flying in all directions. "Without Mr. B., it's all going to change. And I don't want it to change."

"I hate to see Mr. B. go to a nursing home too, but there's nothing we can do about it," said Josie. "We're just kids. Even if we come up with a way Mr. B. can stay here, nobody will listen to us."

"Mr. B. is never going to get to show us the best place to hunt for geodes or where to find the blue thundereggs," Casey said.

"And he will never get to teach me how to be a real rock-hound," Josie added.

Casey sighed. "I know we have to face facts, but I'm not going to let Mr. B. go off to that place before I say goodbye. Even if he can't say anything to us, I want him to know we still care about him."

"Then why don't we go over there and do that very thing?"

They turned to find Myca standing behind them with a big smile on his face. "Toby told me where to find you," he explained. "You ready to go see Mr. B. right now?"

"What are we supposed to do?" Josie put her hands on her hips and looked at Myca with narrowed eyes. "Just walk up and announce we've come to see Mr. B. and march right past Hal as if he weren't there?"

Myca's grin widened. "Something like that. 'Cause he isn't there. He just left Mr. B.'s. I passed him on my way home."

"We don't know how long Hal will be gone," said Casey. "He might have just taken a quick trip to the store."

"Not the way he was all fancied up, with his hair and his beard all combed neat and trim," Myca said, running a hand over his hair and chin. "I could even smell the aftershave lotion when he drove past me. So I don't expect he'll be back real soon."

"I know Mom said not to go, but this might be our last chance to say goodbye to Mr. B.," said Casey. "I think she will understand."

"Count me in," said Josie.

"I'm ready," Myca agreed.

They checked to see if anybody was watching, then angled across the still-warm sand to Mr. B.'s side of the beach. A minute later they were shielded from view by the thick hedge.

Casey started quickly toward the house. "We'll try the front door first," he said, stepping up on the porch.

"What if Hal locked it?" asked Josie.

"Mr. B. keeps a key under a flowerpot on the porch," said Myca.

Casey tapped the brass knocker on the door. "Mr. B.? Mr. B., are you here?" There was no answer.

Josie moved to the window and tried to peek in. "I can't see anything with the drapes closed. Knock again."

Casey rapped harder. He put his ear against the door and listened. Only silence came from inside the house. "I'm going in." He turned the knob. The door was locked. "I'll have to get the key," he said.

"Got it right here," Myca said, dropping it into his hand. Together they tiptoed into the front hall. The living room was deep in shadows. There was enough light to tell Mr. B.'s favorite chair was empty. They moved on to the library. It was empty too.

"Aunt Rose said he was in that little room off the

kitchen," said Josie. "Mr. B. must still be in there."

"If he's not there, we'll try his room upstairs," said Casey, pushing the swinging door back and hurrying across the kitchen.

Myca paused. "Did you hear something?" he whispered.

Casey froze in midstride. Holding his breath, he listened hard. Only thick, heavy silence pressed in around them. Then a board creaked. Casey's heart beat double time.

"It's only the house settling," said Josie in a low voice. "Will you guys stop jumping at shadows?" She crossed the kitchen and tried to open the door to the small room. It was locked too.

"I'll get the key," said Casey. "It's on that rack over there behind the door." Casey handed her the key.

When the door swung open, Josie stopped in the doorway. Casey and Myca looked over her shoulders. Mr. B. was still on the bed, asleep.

"He looks awful!" Myca whispered. "I've never seen Mr. B. looking so bad. Maybe he really is sick, like Hal says."

They moved quietly into the room and up to the bed.

"Mr. B.?" Casey reached out and touched the old man's hand. "Wake up, Mr. B. It's me, Casey." Mr. Beckerman didn't move.

Myca leaned over the bed, close to the still form, and said, "Mr. B., it's us. Wake up." A low moan escaped Mr. Beckerman's lips.

Casey took the old man by the shoulder and shook him gently. "You have to wake up and talk to us, Mr. B." His eyes fluttered open for a second, then closed again.

"It's no use," said Josie. "Hal must have given him something to make him sleep. We'd better go."

They stood clustered around the bed for another minute, each saying their own silent goodbye. They left the room and closed the door quietly behind them. Josie fumbled with the lock.

"Let's go out the back way," said Casey. He moved quickly across the kitchen and out the door before Josie or Myca noticed the tears threatening to spill down his cheeks. He stumbled down the back porch steps and knocked over the trash can, spewing trash in all directions.

"You're making enough noise to wake the dead!" Myca grabbed the can to stop it from rolling. "We better get this picked up quick."

Josie bent and started to scoop up the wrappers and bits of eggshell. "Oh, gross!" she muttered.

"Here, hold this like a dustpan," said Myca, handing her a folded newspaper. "And I'll scoop the stuff up onto it with this one."

Casey was looking for something to use as a scoop when he noticed the corner of a bright green envelope sticking out from under a pile of moldy orange peels. It looked vaguely familiar. He scraped away the orange peels and picked the envelope up by the corner. It was the same envelope they had seen Hal take out of Mr. B.'s mailbox. It looked like a greeting-card envelope. He could feel the card still inside. Mr. B. usually put his cards up on the mantel, where he could look at them.

"What are you doing?" Josie asked when she saw Casey standing there. "You're not supposed to be reading other people's mail."

"I was just looking at this envelope." Casey started to toss it back into the trash can, when he saw the return address. He wiped the front of the envelope off in the grass and studied the postmark.

"Hey, come look at this," he said.

"Yuck!" Josie wrinkled up her nose. "It's smeared with garbage."

"What is it? What did you find?" Myca stepped over the pile of trash and tipped his head to see. "It's just an envelope."

"Not just an envelope," said Casey. "It's a green envelope.

"So what?" said Josie.

"So it might be the answer to a lot of questions," Casey said.

Chapter Fifteen

Two Places at Once

"This is the same envelope we saw Hal take out of Mr. B.'s mailbox." Casey held it out. "Take a look at the return address."

"So it's from Hal. Big deal. Come on, Casey, we haven't got time to fool around," Josie began.

"Now look at the postmark," Casey added.

"It's dated four days ago." Suddenly Myca sucked in his breath. "I get it! How could Hal mail that card from Boston four days ago, when he's been here for almost three weeks!"

"Right!" Casey opened the envelope and peeked inside. "There's something written on the card." He started to pull it out.

"It's against the law to read other people's mail," said Josie.

"It's against the law to open other people's mail," said Myca.

"This card has already been opened," said Casey. "And I'm going to read it." He pulled the card out and unfolded it.

"Who is it from? What does it say? Hurry up and read it out loud." Josie craned her neck, trying to see the words herself.

"OK, OK." Casey started at the beginning again. "It says:

Dear Gramps,

I wish I could be there to spend your birthday with you. But good summer jobs are hard to find, and I'm lucky to have this one. I can't take time off unless it's an emergency.

Next year, after I graduate from college, I'm going to take a month and come spend it with you. I'm looking forward to going for a swim across the lake again. Starting off just as the sun comes up, with you pacing me in the boat the way we used to. I think I can still swim that far.

And I can't wait to go rockhounding again. We could hike up into the hills to that place we found that big thunderegg with the monkey face inside. Remember? We could camp out there for a few days and look for some more. That is, if I can still keep up with you. Tell your rockhound buddies, Casey and Myca, to save some of the good rocks for me.

Write soon,
Love, Hal.

"That doesn't sound like the Hal we know," said Josie, taking the card out of Casey's hand to look at it herself.

"Let me see that card again for a minute," said Casey. He scanned the words quickly. "That's got to be it!"

"Be what?" Josie asked, grabbing the card back again.

Casey stabbed one line with his finger. "See what Hal says right there? He's looking forward to going for a swim across the lake. But when you asked Hal if he was going for a swim, he said he wasn't much of a swimmer."

"And I told you how much he knows about rocks and rockhounding. I asked him about that thunderegg with the monkey face while I was trying to stall him in the workshop. He said he didn't remember where he found it," said Myca.

"The day that Hal came, Mr. B. said he wouldn't have known him if he'd passed Hal on the street," said Casey. "Hal said it was his beard. But what if it's more than that?

There is no way he could have mailed this card from Boston and been here to take it out of the mailbox."

"Are you both thinking what I'm thinking?" asked Josie.

"This guy is not the real Hal," said Myca.

Casey nodded. "That has to be the answer."

"Now it's all beginning to make sense," said Myca. "But how are we going to prove he's not the real Hal?"

"I've been thinking about that too," said Casey. "It will take too long to try to convince the grown-ups that Hal is a phony. By the time we get anybody to believe us, Mr. B.'s house and all of his things will be sold, and he'll be in that nursing home."

"So what are we going to do?" said Josie. "Go to the police?"

"They won't believe us either," Casey said, shaking his head. "But I think I know who will."

"Who?" Josie asked.

"Yeah, who?" Myca echoed, sounding like the twins.

"The real Hal," Casey answered.

"How are we going to do that?" Josie asked. "A letter will never get there in time."

"We'll call him," Casey explained. "Mr. B. must have Hal's number written down somewhere. Come on, let's go look for it." They rushed back up the steps and into the kitchen.

"We'll start in the library," said Casey. "Mr. B. has a roll-top desk in there." They hurried down the hall and into the room. Casey rolled the desk cover up to reveal the desk and the little pigeonholes stuffed with papers. "His address book must be in here somewhere."

"I'll look in the phone book," said Myca. "My mama keeps important numbers written on the inside of the cover."

"Mom keeps ours in the top drawer," said Josie.

Casey picked up the small metal personal directory and ran the pointer up to the letter B. The cover popped open. The only name listed under *B* was Hal Beckerman. "Here it is! It was right here in plain sight. Now all we have to do is call."

"Where are we going to call him from?" asked Josie. "There are too many people at your house to make a private call."

"And I'm not allowed to make any more long-distance calls on our phone," said Myca.

"We'll call from right here," said Casey, reaching for the phone. His hand shook a little as he punched in the numbers.

"What are you going to say?" asked Myca.

"Shhhh, it's ringing!" Casey whispered. On the fourth ring, someone picked up the phone. Casey grinned and gave a thumbs-up sign.

"Hi, this is Hal," a cheerful voice said. Casey opened his mouth, but before he could say Hello, Hal said, "I can't come to the phone right now, but if you will leave your name and number at the sound of the beep, I'll call you back as soon as I can. Be talking to you."

"It's an answering machine!" Casey said, looking at Josie and Myca. "Shall I leave a message?" They both nodded.

The beep sounded loud in Casey's ear. He took a deep breath and said, "This is Casey Hilliard, Mr. B.'s friend. Mr. B. is in really big trouble. There's a guy staying here with Mr. B. who says he's you. He's been here for almost three weeks. Right after he came, Mr. B. got sick. This guy is telling everyone that Mr. B. has been sick for a long time with Alzheimer's disease. We know he was never sick before. But nobody will listen to us, because we're just kids. So, if you are the real Hal Beckerman, you'd better come quick. Day after tomorrow, this guy is going to put Mr. B. in a nursing home and sell his house and all of his furniture. Mr. B. can't do anything about it, because he doesn't know what's going on. We think this guy is giving him stuff to make him sleep all the time."

"Tell him the date and the time," Josie whispered.

"And give him your phone number so he can call back," Myca said.

Casey nodded. "It's 8:45 p.m., August 4. If you want to talk to us, my number is 555-7243." There was another beep, and a second later, the dial tone droned in Casey's ear. With a big sigh of relief, he hung up the phone. "Now all we have to do is wait."

"There is one thing we can do," said Josie. "We can pray that the real Hal gets the message before it's too late."

"Let's do it," Casey said. They all closed their eyes. "Jesus, please help Mr. B. Tell the real Hal to get here quick. Amen."

The tick of the big grandfather clock in the hall sounded loud in the quiet house. For the first time, they noticed that the light had faded until they could barely see each other.

Myca pulled the drapes aside and peeked out. "We better get going," he said. "It's dusk already, and I have to be home by dark."

"Do you think he will call back tonight?" said Josie.

"I hope so." Casey picked up Mr. B.'s birthday card. "We might need this for proof," he said. "Let's look in on Mr. B. one more time before we leave." They moved back down the hall to the kitchen and peeked in on Mr. B. Nothing had changed.

"I wish we didn't have to leave him like this," said Casey.

"I know," said Josie, "but there's nothing else we can do."

Casey closed and locked the door again. They let themselves out through the back door and hurried toward the hole in the hedge.

"I gotta go," said Myca, when they reached the driveway. "My folks will be home soon. If you get a call, be sure to let me know."

"You'll be the first," Casey promised. "See you in the morning."

The kids were all in bed when Casey and Josie came around the house. But they weren't asleep yet. A low murmur of boys' voices came from the tent, and giggles came from the porch.

"Casey, Josie, is that you?" his mother called from the living room when they came into the house. "Where have you been?"

"Just out with Myca," Casey answered.

"It's time to get ready for bed," she said from the doorway.

"Aw, Mom, we don't want to go to bed yet," Casey grumbled. "The little kids are still awake."

"You can stay up for half an hour after you get washed up," his mother agreed. "Then it's off to bed and no arguments."

Casey listened for the phone to ring while he got ready for bed. Then he and Josie sat at the kitchen table and waited.

"What if he isn't there?" said Josie. "What if the Hal at Mr. B.'s really is the real Hal?"

"Don't say that." Casey rested his elbows on the table and his chin in his hands. "If he's the real Hal, then Mr. B. really is sick. I don't even want to think about that."

The phone was still silent when his mother told them it was time for bed. Casey prayed again for Mr. B. and crawled into his sleeping bag. At first, he leaned on one elbow, straining to hear the phone. Then he lay back and listened. He was still waiting when he fell asleep.

The next day, Myca kept watch on Mr. B.'s house with his binoculars. Casey and Josie took turns hanging around the house, jumping to answer the phone each time it rang. Myca reported seeing an auctioneer's truck arrive at Mr. B.'s. Casey and Myca slipped through the hedge in time to see Hal come out of the house and shake hands with a man with a clipboard.

They waited all day. But the phone call never came.

The following morning, Myca reported that the auctioneer's truck had returned with a two-man crew. Casey and Josie rushed to see what was going on. The men had arranged long tables on the front lawn. Before long, they began carrying load after load of things from the house, filling the tables with dishes and knickknacks that had been in Mr. B.'s house for years and years.

"I guess there's no use hoping anymore," said Myca. "Nobody can save Mr. B. now."

"That guy over there must be the real Hal after all," said Casey, handing the binoculars to Josie and turning to walk away.

"Here comes another car," said Josie. "It's probably the people from the nursing home coming to get Mr. B. before the auction starts."

"I thought they would come in an ambulance," said Myca. "Give me the glasses. I want to see Mr. B. when he comes out."

"Let's get closer," said Casey. "I want to hear what Hal tells them." They slipped past the trees and crouched behind a clump of shrubs. Suddenly, Casey didn't want to watch, but he couldn't turn his eyes away. It might be the last time he would see Mr. B.

Chapter Sixteen

Blue Thundereggs

Two men got out of the car and walked toward the house. The older man had broad shoulders and a barrel chest. He was wearing a uniform Casey recognized.

"Hey, that's Sheriff Bloomton!" Casey almost shouted the words.

Myca lifted his binoculars and took a closer look. "It is the sheriff. What's he doing here?"

"Let me see." Josie trained the binoculars on the two men. A second later, she gasped.

"What's happening?" Myca asked "What's wrong?"

She handed him back the glasses. "See the man with the sheriff. He's the one in the picture Mr. B. was carrying the other day." Josie clutched Myca and Casey by the arms and grinned. "It's the real Hal!"

"He sure is," said Myca. "Looks just like his picture too."

"Are you serious?" Casey reached for the glasses. "It is! I already gave up hoping he'd come."

"We all did," said Josie. "But he's here now."

Sheriff Bloomton knocked on the door. Someone opened it, and the two men disappeared inside.

"I wonder what's happening?" said Casey.

A few minutes later, Sheriff Bloomton brought the bearded "Hal" out in handcuffs. The sheriff put him in his car and drove away.

"Did you see that! I can't believe he's really gone." Myca grinned. "Now we don't have to worry about him anymore."

"Now we can go see how Mr. B. is today." Casey stepped out from behind the bushes and hurried toward the house. Josie and Myca were right beside him when he lifted the brass knocker.

The door opened. The real Hal Beckerman stood there for a minute, looking at them. Then he grinned. "Don't tell me, let me guess. You're Casey and you're Myca and you're . . . Josie. Right?" They all nodded.

"I thank God that Gramps has friends like you," said Hal. "If you hadn't called me, Lennie would have gotten away with his rotten scheme to cheat Gramps out of everything he owns. Lennie had everybody convinced he was me. Except you three and Gramps."

"When you didn't call back, he had us convinced too," said Casey.

"I wanted to call, but there wasn't time," said Hal. "I didn't get your message until last night. I called the airport first so I could tell you when I'd be here and found out I barely had time to make the next flight. From the looks of things, I got here just in time."

"Who is that guy?" asked Casey. "How did he know so much about you?"

"His name is Lennie Ferron, and I met him my first year in college. We looked so much alike, people would often mistake him for me, and me for him. Lennie even tricked some of my teachers into giving him my grades for a while. He thought it was funny."

"How did he find out about Mr. B?" Myca asked.

"We got to be friends, even roommates for a while. I told him all about Gramps and me," Hal explained. "After I discovered what a deceitful thief Lennie could be, I ended the friendship. Later Lennie dropped out of college, and I forgot about him. It never occurred to me he would use what he'd learned about Gramps to try to fool him. But Gramps wasn't fooled for long. That's why Lennie gave him sleeping pills."

"I knew he gave Mr. B. something to make him sleep," said Josie.

Hal nodded. "And you kids gave Lennie a big headache. When he first saw the property and antiques here, Lennie planned to stay a lot longer and get the best price for everything. It would have meant a lot more money. But you kids kept coming around asking questions. So to get rid of you, he tried to convince you Gramps was a secret drinker, but that didn't work. Then he started a rock slide while you were hiking."

"He did! I knew there was something funny about that," said Myca.

Hal nodded. "He hoped to upset your parents so they would ground you. That didn't work either. So Lennie decided it was time to take what he could get, and get out. And you spoiled that plan too. Gramps is lucky to have friends like you."

"Is he all right?" asked Casey.

"Can we see him?" asked Myca.

"Not yet," said Hal. "Gramps is still asleep. It's going to take a while for the pills to wear off."

It was the next afternoon before Mr. B. was his old self again. Hal invited Casey and Myca and Josie over to see him.

"Hal told me what the three of you did," said Mr. B. "Without your help, I would have lost everything. I can't tell you how grateful I am."

"But Gramps and I have thought of a way to show you," said Hal. Mr. Beckerman's blue eyes twinkled. "How would the three of you like to go on a real rockhounding expedition—a three-day camping trip up into the Ochoco Mountains?"

Casey gasped. "Where the blue thundereggs are?"

Mr. B. chuckled. "That's the place. We'll make a few stops on the way to look for geodes, for you, Myca. And, Josie, a trip like this will give you a really good start on your collection."

"That would be great," said Casey, "but I'm not sure we can go."

"It's all arranged with your parents," said Hal. "And Libby has agreed to come along to keep Josie company."

Casey had a hunch Hal's good looks had something to do with Aunt Libby's decision. "When do we leave?" he asked.

"Tomorrow morning," said Mr. B. "I want to get an early start."

"Tomorrow!" Casey and Myca and Josie yelled at the same time. "We'll be ready!"

And they raced home to pack.